HALFWAY DOWN
PADDY LANE

HALFWAY DOWN PADDY LANE

by Jean Marzollo

The Dial Press / New York

Published by The Dial Press
1 Dag Hammarskjold Plaza
New York, New York 10017

Library of Congress Cataloging in Publication Data

Marzollo, Jean. Halfway down Paddy Lane.

Summary: Fifteen-year-old Kate finds herself transported
back in time to 1850 in her Connecticut town,
where she must adjust to the prejudices against Irish immigrants,
working long hours in a cotton mill, and, tragically,
falling in love with a boy who believes he is her brother.
[1. Space and time—Fiction. 2. Irish Americans—Fiction.
3. United States—Social life and customs—
1783–1865—Fiction] I. Title.
PZ7.M3688Hal [Fic] 80–25854
ISBN 0–8037–3329–1

To Ruth Palmer Smith Martin,
my mother

Acknowledgments

I would like to thank several historians for their help with this book: Caroline Sloat, researcher, Old Sturbridge Village, Sturbridge, Massachusetts; Stephen Victor, curator, Slater Mill Historic Site, Pawtucket, Rhode Island; and Barry O'Connell, associate professor, American Studies and English, Amherst College, Amherst, Massachusetts.

Many friends read the manuscript at its various stages and I am grateful to them, especially: John Savage, Rosemary Wells, Mary Pope Osborne, Irene Trivas, Bonnie Harris, Baxter Harris, Kathleen MacDonald, Kristin O'Connell, Susan Jeffers, Nan Rich, Carol Carson, Larry Alson, David Bynes, Sunny Rhodes, Tania MacNeil, and Elisabeth Martin. Ralph Brill contributed continued interest and materials about industrial archaeology.

I want to thank my husband, Claudio, for his many helpful readings of the text; my agent, Shelly Fogelman, for his steadfast reassurance; Phyllis Fogelman, for encouraging me to write my first novel; and most of all, my editor, Amy Ehrlich, who understood the book before I did.

Our birth is but a sleep and a forgetting.

WILLIAM WORDSWORTH
"Intimations of Immortality"

HALFWAY DOWN
PADDY LANE

1

Kate didn't turn or open her eyes. It was as if only her mind had awakened. Something's changed, she thought. Something's wrong.

Lifting her eyelids just enough to focus, she saw a room she didn't recognize. Was she visiting someone? It had happened to her before, waking up in someone's house and momentarily forgetting where she was, but this was different. No one she knew lived in a place like this.

Cautiously Kate opened her eyes further, looking around the room for clues that would explain the feeling she had of being in the wrong place. There was only one window, and it was small and square. The ceiling slanted as if the room were in an attic. Attic. Of course.

With a groan Kate turned over and buried her face in the pillow. She remembered now. It was the first morning in the new house. Old house, rather. The thought of waking up in such a cramped and creepy room every single day all summer long made her feel sick.

Kate wished she were back in her *real* house, in her *real* room. Eyes shut, she could see it so clearly, she could practically count the little blue flowers on the wallpaper. She could see sunlight pouring through the white curtains on the windows. She could see her posters, the desk she had painted blue, and her blue and yellow pinstriped comforter.

Why, Kate wondered for the hundredth time, when they had a perfectly nice, normal house, did her mother get the crazy idea of buying a little old one on the other side of town and moving into it for the summer?

"It will be an adventure into history!" her mother had said with a dangerous, manic glow in her eyes. "We'll rent our house and live in the old one for the summer. We'll fix it up and put it on the market in the fall. You'll see, Kate, you'll just love it! It will be like a vacation because everything will be so different and interesting."

Well, that was the limit. It was one thing to have a mother who hung pictures of her ancestors on the dining room walls and talked about them all the time. "This is your great-grandfather on your *father's* side, and this is your great-grandmother on *my* side." Et cetera. Et cetera. At least all Kate had to do was pretend to listen. It was another thing altogether to have a mother who made her whole family move across town because it was "interesting."

The trouble had started when her mother, who loved antiques and old houses, had decided to make her interests "economically viable." All she could talk about was rehabilitating (or "rehabbing," as she put it) old houses for a profit. Kate thought that actually moving to the old house in North Lancaster was going too far and assumed her father would feel that way too. But he said he thought it was a terrific idea. He would help, he added. He had a month's vacation coming and looked forward to doing something "physical."

So as usual Kate had no choice. At fifteen she didn't want to go to camp anymore, and she was too young to get a job. Her parents offered to pay an hourly rate for the time she put in on the old house, so at least she supposed she would earn some money for school clothes. But it was going to be a miserable, boring summer.

All her friends from South Lancaster were going away and she didn't know anyone over here. An adventure into history, my eye. What was she supposed to do? Learn about history from sagging walls and old purple wallpaper?

Wait . . . a . . . minute, thought Kate. Her heart froze. Oh, my God. When she opened her eyes, the walls were gray. She forced herself to look again. It was true. Instead of the ugly old wallpaper with purple lilacs on it, which she distinctly remembered from the night before, the walls around her were covered with grimy gray plaster.

Terrified, Kate sat up. She was wearing a thin cotton slip. Where was the pink nylon nightie she'd worn to bed? She looked around in panic and noticed for the first time that there was another bed in the room. Both beds had thin quilts on them and rough, patched sheets seamed in the middle. There were two pillows on each bed. The purple wallpaper was absolutely gone.

She held her breath and stared at the furniture. The bureau she had unpacked her clothes into the day before was missing, but the little table with the marble top was still there. That was where she had set up her stereo.

It was gone. Her stereo! She'd been robbed!

"Mother!" she screamed.

"She's leaving," someone yelled from downstairs.

"Wait for me!" Kate called, jumping out of bed. Running wildly around, she saw a wooden trunk at the foot of her bed. Jerking it open, she found it filled with neatly folded antique clothes. She ran to check the trunk at the foot of the other bed. Same thing.

Okay, Kate told herself, pressing her hand flat on her chest. Be cool. There's got to be an explanation for this.

She made herself think. I know where I am. I'm in a house on Patricia Lane in North Lancaster, Connecticut. I'm *sure* this is the same room I moved my stuff into yesterday and went to sleep in last night. But everything here is old-fashioned so . . . so the only explanation is that I'm dreaming.

Kate's panic began to subside. Yes, she reassured herself, it's a dream, and not such a bad one at that. I've had dreams before in which worse things happened.

Kate knelt and looked in the trunk again. I could try these clothes on, she thought with delight. Carefully she lifted out a small ivory comb, another slip like the one she was wearing, two pairs of white cotton pantaloons, four unattached white collars, two long aprons, three petticoats, and a pair of long white cotton knit stockings. Underneath were two folded dresses: a reddish brown calico and a light gray wool plaid with black ribbon trim. Kate held them up one at a time. Both had tight bodices, long sleeves, and long, gathered skirts. Although Kate preferred the colors in the gray dress, she decided to put the brown one on because it was the same color as her hair, her best feature. Her face was all right, but people always remarked about her hair, which was chestnut color, naturally wavy, and long.

Kate folded the gray dress and gently set it back in the trunk. Spreading the brown one out on the bed, she noticed with a moment's regret that it was a little dirty and worn looking, but she didn't really care. It was still lovely.

Kate felt giddy. She put her hands above her head and did a little twirl in the space next to the bed. I love this dream, she thought. It's like a ballet. Only there's one thing wrong. Kate stopped. She couldn't put it off any longer. She absolutely *had* to go to the bathroom.

On the little marble table where her stereo should have been was a white pitcher and a bowl. Kate had been dragged by her mother to enough historical museums to know they were for washing up. Kate looked inside the pitcher. Sure enough, it was filled with water. She knelt down on her hands and knees, peeked under the bed, and saw what she hoped to see: a chamber pot. She pulled it out, lifted the top off, sat down on the cold round rim, and used it. This is the most realistic dream I've ever had, she thought with a shiver. She put the lid on the pot and slowly pushed it back under the bed, wondering with a nervous giggle if anyone in her dream would ever empty it.

Kate stood up and tried to get back into her ballet mood. The linen pantaloons fit perfectly, which helped, but she couldn't find a bra anywhere. Finally she gave up and decided to keep the slip on and just go braless. She chose a petticoat with six rows of thick white cording sewn around the hem. The cording, Kate guessed, was supposed to make the petticoat stick out, but it didn't work very well.

Now for the dress. Kate pulled the brown one over her head and felt it fall into position around her waist perfectly.

There was a small mirror on the wall. Standing on tiptoe, she looked into it and thought with satisfaction that the dress made her waist look thin and her breasts look bigger. Kate did a pirouette. I feel like Scarlett O'Hara in *Gone With the Wind*, she thought. Except that Scarlett's skirt stuck out farther. Impulsively Kate pulled the other two petticoats up under her skirt and buttoned them at the waist. Yes, that was much better.

"Hurry up!"

She was twirling around on her tiptoes when she heard the voice. It was her dad, probably calling her for breakfast, but Kate was not ready to awaken so she twirled away from his voice and ran back to the bed. She had seen a pair of shoes and a floral-printed hatbox underneath. Just let me finish this dream, Daddy! Let me get completely dressed, she thought, rushing. But the shoes were a big disappointment. Not only were they flat and ugly like boys' shoes, they were also too tight. Peevishly Kate took them off and threw them on the floor. She looked through both trunks for something prettier but couldn't find a thing.

"In God's holy name, what are y' waiting for?"

For the first time she heard the voice clearly. It was not her father at all. It was a deep voice, not the voice of anyone she knew. It had an accent.

"Daddy," she whispered. Her heart started to pound. The thought that her mother and father might not be downstairs suddenly occurred to her. But this is only a dream, she reminded herself, blocking the fear that was growing inside her chest. If I don't like it, all I have to do is wake up. As a matter of fact, I think that's just exactly what I'm going to do this very minute.

Kate stood up and pinched herself on her left arm. Nothing happened. Her heart started to pound louder, yet for some peculiar reason, all Kate could think of were the flat, ugly shoes. If she had only been able to find a dressy pair, she would have felt more prepared.

"Hasten, Kate, fetch your bonnet and gloves and come! It's our turn next!"

Whoever belonged to the voice knew her name. And to make matters worse, somewhere in the house a clock started to strike. God! Kate pinched herself harder, then harder again, almost breaking the skin with her fingernails. When for a third time nothing happened, Kate grew so afraid that she couldn't think. A white blank closed in around her ears. She tried to swallow, but her mouth was too dry.

"Kate!"

The urgency in the voice made her focus. She had to do something! Tearing open the hatbox, she grabbed the bonnet and gloves inside. The hat was made of straw with a wide brim and colored ribbons that Kate tied under her chin as fast as she could. The gloves were made of thin tan leather. They couldn't possibly be real, she thought, yanking them on. Forcing herself to take a deep breath, she grabbed the shoes, stood up, opened the door, and stumbled out into a small dark landing at the top of a narrow stairway.

"KATE!"

"I'm ready," she said in an abnormally high voice. Ready for what? she wondered hysterically, just as a boy with a black suit and thick black hair appeared at the bottom of the stairs. He was tall with broad shoulders and a muscular chest that strained the buttons on his jacket. His hair wasn't cut by a barber, that was obvious. Chunks of it fell halfway down his ears. Above his forehead, though, it was combed back neatly. In fact, it still seemed wet. The boy's eyes were blue. He was staring at her.

"Ah, Kate," he said, looking at her feet. "You mean to tell me your shoes still hurt? Here, let me help you." He bounded up the stairs three at a time and stood right next to her.

"Well now, where's the shoehorn?" he asked with a sudden, lovely grin.

Kate couldn't speak. In spite of his odd haircut, he was the most handsome boy she'd ever seen.

"Never ye mind, I'll fetch it," he said, and with that he bounded back down the stairs, grabbed something from a downstairs room, and bounded up again. He talked just like her great-grandmother Moira used to talk. That meant he must be Irish.

"Well, what are y' waiting for?" he asked, grinning that grin again. "Sit down."

Kate thought she would faint. She was sure if she tried to sit, she would fall, but somehow the moment of panic passed, and she did sit, as nonchalantly as she possibly could. The boy sat down too, pressing right up against her because the stairwell was so narrow. He could use a deodorant, Kate thought, and then felt silly to be thinking such thoughts when she didn't even know who he was or what on earth was going on.

What in the world *was* going on? Kate felt the walls spin around her as the boy reached across her lap and picked up one of her feet. He put it gently on his left knee. Kate focused. The spinning stopped. She noticed that the sleeves of his suit were frayed. His shirt cuff was hand stitched. His hands were rough. His fingernails were clean. He was using a plain ivory shoehorn to slip her shoes on.

If Kate had been able to think complete thoughts, she might have said to herself, "He's nice," or "He's poor," or "He's very different from Warren." As it was, she couldn't even think enough to say thank you. Before she knew it, the boy was finished and back downstairs, peeking out the front door.

It was the same short door as the one in the house they had just moved into, only now it wasn't blue; it was bare wood. The hall and the stairs were the same shape she remembered from the night before.

"Now!" he said.

She was so determined to walk downstairs gracefully that she did. Just like in the movies, her long dress swirled along as her feet, though pinched by the strange shoes, stepped delicately down the stairs. It was not easy because the steps were narrow and steep, but somehow Kate managed, feeling rather proud of herself. She was suddenly glad she hadn't awakened. Apparently this was a good dream after all.

At the bottom of the stairs she saw the boy's elbow extended out to her, so she did what came naturally. She slipped her left arm through his and walked with him out the front door.

Whew! The first thing she became aware of was the

warm, acrid odor of fresh horse manure. There were several piles of it lying in the middle of the dirt road in front of the house. The boy didn't seem to think anything of this as he and Kate stepped around the piles and started walking down the middle of the road.

2

Kate was too astonished to talk. There were no cars, no streetlights, and no telephone poles. The dirt road was rutted and bumpy. There were no sidewalks. Wondering what year she was dreaming about, Kate guessed 1900 for no particular reason. Although she knew enough about history to recognize a chamber pot when she saw one, she didn't know much about dates.

The house she had just come from was in the middle of a row of eight houses, all exactly alike: small, square wooden cottages in need of paint. On the other side of the street was a meadow that made Kate wish she'd looked more closely at Patricia Lane. It was like this but different. Vaguely she remembered that across the street had been a small garden apartment, some houses, a parking lot, and an A&P.

A rooster crowed behind a house and was answered by another rooster farther down. Kate thought she heard a cow moo but wasn't sure. Under her hand the boy's arm muscles tightened and relaxed. Without moving her head, she strained her eyes to the side to look at him. He seemed to be talking to himself. Since he was paying no attention to her whatsoever, she turned her head more. His skin was pale and absolutely clear.

She couldn't help comparing him with Warren, her boyfriend. Warren was cute, but his straight blond hair always fell in his face and made his forehead break out. Warren was Kate's size. When they danced close, their ears touched. This boy was about six inches taller. Warren was sixteen; this boy was about eighteen, Kate guessed.

"Uncle Mick's not going to like what I have to say about the turnout," the boy blurted out, "but I've made up me mind, Kate."

Kate stared at him incomprehensively. He seemed so . . . real.

"What ails ye, Kate?" he asked. "Y' look as white as the moon."

"Do—do you know me?" Kate said. She hadn't exactly planned to ask that question because, after all, this was a dream, and in a dream anyone might know her, but the question had slipped out anyway, and there it was.

"What did y' say?"

"I said . . . I mean, how do you know my name?"

"Why are you talking that way?"

"You mean my speech? That's what I'm trying to figure out. Why is yours so different? Is it because this is a dream?"

The boy's eyebrows lowered. "Are y' daft, Kate? To joke on a morning like this?"

"I'm not joking," she said. "It's just that this dream gives me a really weird feeling."

"Really weird?" he said, mimicking her. "I never heard such words." He started walking faster, as if to ignore her silliness, but Kate reached out and pulled his sleeve.

"It's almost as if I'm in another time!" she said.

The expression on the boy's face got worse. Before he had looked merely annoyed, but now he looked horrified.

"Lord have mercy!" he shouted, looking around quickly to see if anyone heard. "What would Ma say if she heard you joking like this before Mass? Shame on ye, Kate!"

The expression on his face was so fierce that Kate looked down. She felt her throat swell and ache.

"What do y' expect me to think, Kate," said the boy impatiently. "That you have brain fever like Old Man Flynn? Do y' want to be chained up in a barn like him? Fed with the pigs? Keep talking like that and ye will be!"

Kate didn't say any more.

"I say, Kate! Look at me!"

She looked up, biting her lip.

The boy let his breath out audibly and seemed to notice for the first time how truly frightened she was.

"God love y', Kate, here we are arguing in the road when they're all waiting for us. I'm sorry to be so upset, but I've been jittery as a linden tree all morning, worrying about the Mass and the turnout."

He seemed to relax, and he grinned the same lovely way he had at the foot of the stairs. It was like the sun coming out from behind a cloud. They started walking again. When they reached the end of the road, they turned right onto another road. This one had no houses on it, just pasture on the left and trees on the right. Kate tried desperately to calm down and think clearly. Neither she nor the boy spoke.

"Patrick!"

The shout came from the right, from the woods. So his name is Patrick, Kate thought.

"Over here!"

They walked quickly into the woods and saw a sandy-haired boy about Patrick's age standing behind a tree. Patrick dropped Kate's arm and ran over.

"James," he said, "what happened?"

"They were waiting on Hartford Road. When Father Tully rode by, they stoned him!" James had an Irish accent too.

"Who?"

"No one saw them, but it must have been the Know-Nothings."

"Aye. Mary, Mother of God! Is he dead?"

"Nae, but he caught a nasty rock on the side of the head. He's bleeding, but he'll be saying Mass this morning anyway."

"Do y' think he can?"

"He's determined."

"Ah. Do they know where the Mass is? Did they follow them?"

"I don't think so. Father Tully told his driver to take him to Flaherty's. When they got there, the driver carried him in as if he were unconscious."

"Good."

"We don't think they'll be watching Hennigan's house anyway. Everyone knows Mick hasn't been in a church for twenty years. And even if they were watching, what would they see? People have been arriving in twos and threes since dawn, never enough to attract anyone's attention."

"Aye, that's the truth of it. Then cut through the woods, James, and tell everyone to wait. We'll take the road as planned and be along in a minute."

"But see here, Patrick, do y' think you should tell your uncle to call this off? I'd hate to see Hennigan beaten like Murray was last month."

"Uncle Mick has a right to hold a Mass at his house if he wants to, Know-Nothings be damned. This is America, isn't it?"

"Aye," said James resolutely. He turned for a second and looked at Kate's hair. He didn't say a word, but Kate had the feeling he was impressed. Wondering if Patrick felt the same way, she put her hands up and fluffed it in the back. But James ran off and Patrick wasn't paying any attention to her. Instead he was watching James with a worried look on his face. These boys were so serious! Kate sighed, feeling confused.

Patrick glanced both ways down the road to see if anyone was coming. There was no one so they started walking again. Patrick's face was set and angry, but he said nothing.

Stoning a priest! What an odd thing to dream about.

They turned right onto another dirt road with more cottages. Ten of them this time, exactly the same as the ones on the other road. Patrick stopped.

"Now then," he said abruptly. "Go on in. I'm going to get Nora at her boardinghouse."

Dream or no dream, Kate didn't want to be left alone.

"What's the matter *now*, Kate? Are ye feeling sorely about your hair? Truth be told, it doesn't look so bad. Sure, when I first saw you at the top of the stairs, I almost didn't recognize you, but I said to myself, well, what do y' know? My sister Kate has grown up independent. Now go in before anyone sees us loitering here and gets suspicious."

Sister? Did he say "sister"? Did he think he was her brother? Kate was dazed. She watched him turn and walk away with a sense of mission she didn't understand. She watched him reach the end of the road, turn, and disappear.

Now she was conspicuously, horribly alone. She looked

at the house she was supposed to enter, and as she did, she was aware of every detail as if she were looking through a magnifying glass. She saw the rough stone slab used for a front step, she saw the bare spots on the whitewashed clapboards, she saw ripples in the glass windows. She smelled the strong, sweet smell of honeysuckle and heard a woodpecker in the trees. Her hands were sweating. She wiped them on her dress, and as she did, she felt every cotton thread in the rough fabric. Goose bumps spread across her back.

This isn't a dream, she suddenly knew. That boy was real. That house is real. This dress is real. Maybe I've changed places in history with another girl named Kate. But I look exactly like her, and when I go in that house, people are going to expect me to be her.

Fear squeezed Kate's ribs and held them tight. She didn't want to stand in the middle of the road any longer, but she didn't know what else to do. She thought of running but didn't know where to run to. She knew that down the street, over the hill, wherever she ran, she was still going to be in the past. Kate shuddered. For a long time she stood still, trying to think what to do about a nightmare that was true.

Finally she felt an ounce of bravery and common sense return. This will not last, she told herself as adamantly as she could. I have slipped through time in an instant and in another instant I'll slip back. Meanwhile I must act calm and try to fit in here. I can't go around telling everyone I'm from 1981. They'll think I'm crazy. If Warren told me he was from the year 3000, I'd stop seeing him.

Kate hitched up her skirts and made herself walk down the path to the front door. There didn't appear to be anything going on inside, but that, she supposed, was because this Mass, or whatever it was, was intended to be secret. There were people in there who would know *why* it was a secret. Now, who would they be? Kate tried to think logically. A mother, Patrick had mentioned. An uncle named Mick. Hennigan, James had called him. Mick Hennigan. This was his house. He and the mother would talk to Kate as if she were Patrick's sister.

But as Kate reached up to knock on the door, her stomach turned over like a half-dead fish. Her fears had overwhelmed her again, so completely, she was afraid to breathe. She was afraid that if she moved her chest, she would throw up.

"Hello, Kate, come right in," whispered someone, cracking open the door to let her in. A friendly, squinting, white-haired man in a faded black suit pointed her toward a doorway on the other side of a small kitchen. Numb, Kate crossed the room and stepped into a musty parlor filled with many chairs, a sofa, a bed, and about two dozen people.

Some of the men had beards. The women and girls in the room were dressed in long dresses just like Kate's, and all of them had their hair tied back in tight buns. Kate started to break out in an itchy, embarrassed sweat.

"Kate!" whispered a thin, half-toothless woman sitting on a rocking chair. The woman had stopped praying but was holding her rosary beads poised in the air, ready to go on. "Come here," she said, coughing.

Embarrassed, Kate crossed the room, nodding as politely as she could to everybody. The woman who had spoken was trying to stop coughing now. She sounded awful. She could have been sixty if you judged by her teeth and gray hair. She could have been thirty if you judged by her figure. It was hard to tell. Finally, after great effort, she cleared her throat and said, "Why did you wear your hair that way?" Her voice was weak but authoritative. Her manner was both possessive and kind. Kate knew instantly. This woman is Patrick's mother. She thinks she's mine too. She's got that attitude, like she owns me.

Kate looked quickly around the room. Everyone was looking at her and waiting for her answer.

"I, um, I, uh." Oh, God. Patrick's words about brain fever came back to her. In ninth grade her class had studied how the insane were treated long ago. They were cared for like beasts, she remembered, chained, locked up in cages or stalls, and fed garbage.

I've got to speak with an Irish accent right now, she said to herself, or else they'll think I'm crazy. She thought of her great-grandmother's lilting voice and wished she hadn't died when Kate was eight. She tried to remember Patrick's phrases. An eternity passed while she forced her memory to work. I've got to get this right, she said to herself.

"I, uh, I've been jittery as a linden tree all morning," she finally said.

"Aye?" said Patrick's mother.

"Worrying about the Mass and the turnout."

Someone laughed quietly behind Kate. It sounded like a girl. Kate didn't dare look around. She didn't know what a turnout was and hoped no one would ask her about it. Someone else laughed. As Patrick's mother glanced around the room she must have sensed amusement, not derision, because her face softened.

"Ye mean you were too worried to comb your hair? Saints alive, I never heard of such a thing," she whispered, looking at her rosary again. When Kate was sure the woman had resumed praying, she stepped over to an empty chair in the corner and sat down. Folding her hands in her lap, Kate felt amazed, relieved, and unbearably hot.

3

After a few disquieting minutes during which Kate
thought she would never stop sweating, she lifted her eyes
to look around the room. With relief she found that except for one girl about twelve years old across the room,
no one was paying attention to her anymore. The girl
looked tired, much too tired for her age, yet there was
something comical about her face, something about the
tiredness that was exaggerated, like on a clown's face.
Suddenly the girl made a funny face that prompted Kate
to giggle. But when the man next to the girl glowered

fiercely, first at her and then at Kate, both girls sobered immediately. Kate looked away.

Two people sat on the bed. The farther one, a huge, ruddy, red-bearded man leaning against the headboard, appeared to be asleep. An old lady sat at the other end with her shoulders so rounded over that she looked as if she were about to somersault onto the floor.

More people were coming. It was Patrick with a beautiful young woman. Nodding to everyone in the room, the two of them sat down in the middle of the sofa.

Was this Nora? Was she a sister too? Somehow Kate knew she wasn't. She had light auburn hair, hazy green eyes, and remarkably creamy skin that made Kate despise her own freckles. When she noticed Kate staring at her, she smiled, moving her lips to say hello.

Kate smiled back, but she felt awful. Her antique underwear prickled, and she caught an unpleasant whiff of her own body odor. Not that it mattered. The whole room smelled sour.

Someone else was coming, a frail, balding priest with a bandaged head and a gold-embroidered shawl over his shoulders. Greeted by small cries and whispers of shock, he glanced around the room, too dazed to manage more than a nod of greeting. Everyone including Kate watched intently as he set a small black leather case down on the floor. Kate was surprised that he wore a regular black suit instead of a priest's suit.

She didn't know much about priests. When she was little, she had gone to a Catholic church with her mother, but then mysteriously their weekly practice was discontinued. Over the years when Kate had asked why, her mother said that all religions were worthwhile and that Kate could pick any one she wanted when she grew older. After a few years Kate had no longer considered herself a Catholic. When she went to the pool, she even stopped crossing herself on the diving board like real Catholic kids.

The priest opened his case and with shaking hands took out a chalice, a cloth, and a small silver plate. He was so frail and thin that he gave off an ancient feeling, heightened by his injury. Kate wished someone would help him but no one did. They watched in silence and then, as if on cue, got down on their knees and began to pray quietly in Latin.

Kate copied them. When they crossed themselves, she crossed herself. When they stood up, she stood up. When they mumbled, she mumbled.

The bandage on the priest's head was getting bloodier, not so bloody that it actually dripped, but it was definitely getting soggy.

Slowly he started moving around the room. Oh, no! thought Kate with a gasp. I can't take Communion. I haven't been to Confession in years. But when the priest got to her, she shut her eyes and swallowed the small round host with a dry, guilty gulp. She heard the priest move on and opened her eyes. No one was looking at her except Patrick's mother, and she quickly looked away.

The priest was now at the front of the room. "My dear

friends," he said in a voice so quiet, Kate had to strain to hear. "We must keep in mind always, no matter what happens, that the glory of God is stronger than the hatred of the Devil. It may not seem so sometimes but I truly know it is."

The priest continued, his voice getting louder and stronger with each word. "Despite our enemies the Church will survive in America. Now, God bless each one of you, and God bless the Irish people, all of them, those in the old country and those here in our new land. 'Tis a fine country with work for everyone. Ye must be brave. Amen."

"Amen," said everyone in the room except Kate. "Amen," she echoed quickly, surprised to find a lump in her throat. She looked again at Patrick. He was cracking his knuckles and seemed to be thinking of something else.

The Mass seemed to have given the priest strength. Even though his head must have been throbbing, he smiled, raised his hands in benediction, and intoned the final blessing of the Mass.

Relief spread through the room as everyone stood up and greeted one another.

Kate didn't know what was going on, but in spite of her ignorance she sensed happiness in the room, and something about the frail priest's blessing had touched her and made her feel safe.

"Kate, you look so funny!" It was the tired girl who'd been sitting across the room. "Come, let's go outside and talk."

Kate shook her head no. She didn't know why. Maybe it was because the girl was younger and consequently the first person Kate had spoken to who wasn't intimidating.

"Nae? Well now, I suppose you're right, Kate. Say, what do you think of Nora? Doesn't she look beautiful today? Do you think she and Patrick will be getting married when the church is finished?"

Patrick and Nora married. What a ridiculous idea. They were much too young. Kate was disgusted with this wimpy little girl for making the suggestion and almost said so. Luckily the huge, red-bearded man, wide-awake now, was making an announcement from the corner of the bed. Everyone sat back down.

Kate figured he was Uncle Mick by his apology for not cleaning up the house better. "Praise God, as far as we know, we've not been noticed here," he said. He glanced at Patrick and his friends standing in the doorway to the kitchen. "And as far as we know, the rock that hit Father Tully will be returned to its sender this evening."

Uncle Mick's eyes twinkled when he said this, and many of the men and boys laughed under their breath conspiratorially. Kate sensed a feeling of revenge among them and wondered if Patrick would be involved.

Uncle Mick continued. "Now then, I have spoken with Mr. Lancaster. He says to report to work tomorrow as usual. He says not to worry about the Yankees staying home. The mill will be open under new regulations whether the Yankees like it or not. And it will be guarded, he told me. The new agent, Mr. Harris, has taken care of everything. He said he's already sent to Ireland for more workers to take the place of the troublemakers."

"Hold on, Uncle," said Patrick abruptly. He stood up, flushed and awkward. "Now y' know I don't like the Yankees and sure I want to bring over my relatives, but I've been thinking. I believe we too should turn out with the Yanks tomorrow."

"Nae!" shouted practically everyone in the room. Patrick put up his hands to quell their protests and raised his voice.

"I tell y', the new agent, this Mr. Harris ye mentioned, he's been hired for one thing only—to increase profits. Can't y' see? Now that there are so many of us here, everything is changing. Woe be to us if we can't see that it's always going to change for the worse. The Yanks want to show Mr. Harris they can't be pushed around. We should turn out too, to show him that he can't push the Irish around either. We're not machines, Mick."

"Patrick," said Uncle Mick tensely, "all that the new agent has done is cut out the morning break. Fifteen minutes, Patrick. That's all. We still have breakfast, dinner, and supper."

Several voices murmured agreement.

"Maybe so," Patrick replied angrily, "but you just wait. If we don't show our strength, in a few months he'll speed up the looms. Then what are we going to do? Don't y' see, man? He knows we can't stop working like the Yankees. We don't have farms to go home to."

Patrick sat down in a huff. Everyone was in a huff.

For a moment no one spoke, and Kate felt sorry for Patrick.

"Mr. Lancaster wouldn't have hired an agent so wicked," said someone finally. "After all, it was he who sold us the land for our church, wasn't it?"

Patrick laughed. "Aye, and he made a good bargain when he did it. Sure, I know Mr. Lancaster has always seemed decent, but I tell ye, he's hired Mr. Harris to do his dirty work."

"But if we turn out, Patrick," said James, "what will we do for money? And board and food?"

Someone else said, "The little money we've set aside is to bring over our mother. We can't spend it to keep ourselves alive."

"But don't you see," Patrick said impatiently, "that is exactly what the new agent is counting on: that we'll work no matter what he does. That makes us no better than the slaves in the South who pick the cotton we spin and weave."

"Ah, Patrick," said Nora calmly, as if she were used to soothing him, "no one owns us now, do they? You've no more chance of persuading us to strike with the Yankees than you've got of roasting a potato in the Irish Sea. Won't ye give up, man?"

Patrick glowered at her, and Kate was pleased.

"Don't be putting yourself out so," Nora continued in a responsible voice. "Aye, we live in company houses and we shop at the company store. You may call this 'stuck,' but we call it a decent way to make a living. So the new agent took away our morning break. Fifteen minutes more work a day in America is nothing compared to starving in Ireland, and there are plenty of people in this room, Patrick, who never want to do that again. America's the best poor man's country in the world."

Patrick looked at the ceiling and sighed. He held his body tense and separate from Nora's.

Uncle Mick tried to appease him. "For God's sake, lad, the Yankees hate us. Don't they say we're ignorant Paddies who care only for drinking? Don't they call our street Paddy Lane? Begorra, they stoned our priest this morning! Tell me, what do y' want to take their side for?"

"Only this time, Mick," Patrick said angrily. "Sure, up to now there's been no real trouble between us, aye? Ah, yes, I know, a couple of drunken brawls and plenty of insults, God knows, but this turnout, man, it gives us a chance for a common ground."

"Who wants a common ground?" asked James. "We can take care of ourselves."

"Maybe so," said Patrick, "but the turnout is going to change things. If the Yankees stay home and we take their jobs, they'll hate us more than ever. More of them will join the Know-Nothing party to try to get rid of us. Just when our church is getting finished, I say 'tis a shame to cause trouble, especially when it will hurt *us* in the end. Why, we could fight against the new agent if we worked *with* them. To be sure, we'll never get anywhere on our own."

But Patrick was smoldering with ideas no one wanted

to hear. Kate wished at least one person would agree with him, but no one did. His ideas seemed logical to her, but she didn't dare say a word.

"Don't y' see—" he shouted, but this time his mother coughed and started to speak.

"Hush, Pat," she said. "We have no choice. If we turn out, we'll just be replaced by others like ourselves. And then we'll have to separate. Perhaps you could get work on canals, perhaps Kate and Clare could do domestic work; but God knows what will happen to the rest of us." She stopped for a moment, then went on. "All your father ever wanted was a home and church in America, God rest his soul, but he didn't live long enough to see it. Now you be quiet, Pat. Your father in Heaven and God Almighty will help us. Y' must have faith, and we must stay together."

Furious but stopped, Patrick looked down at the floor. He didn't say another word. He reminded Kate of herself. She, too, fumed when she got mad.

"Well now," said Uncle Mick quickly with some embarrassment. "I suggest y' leave as y' came with the person y' came with. Take all the time you want so that none of our Yankee 'friends' who happen to be riding by will notice anything going on. There are scones and tea in the kitchen. Help yourselves. I'm sorry there's not more, but I gave half my wages last month to bring in the stained-glass windows."

A few people chuckled—partly, Kate guessed, because they knew Uncle Mick wasn't religious and partly to lift the mood in the room. Everyone got up, relieved to be off the subject of the turnout.

"Wait, everybody." It was the white-haired man who had let her in. "I'm passing the hat for the Irish Relief Association, but I must remind you as you give so generously that our church isn't quite finished yet. I'm asking y' to give a little extra if ye can, half for the victims of the famine and half for our church. Sure, I know I told you before we had enough money to finish, but now, me friends, it seems we need four dollars more to pay on the delivery of the last stained-glass window. I know you haven't got much, but every penny counts."

He passed a hat to the woman on his right and smiled as she proudly put a coin in and passed it on. "If we can raise the money today and everything goes on schedule, we'll be celebrating Mass in our new church next Sunday!"

Everyone cheered. Even Kate, who didn't know exactly what the man was talking about, felt excited by the general enthusiasm. She saw Patrick's mother take money out of a small purse and put it in the hat as it went by.

"And how's the altar cloth coming, Mrs. O'Hara?" the white-haired man asked.

Patrick's mother beamed. "Surely it's the grandest lace I ever made," she said.

O'Hara, Kate thought. O'Hara. Patrick O'Hara. Kate O'Hara.

4

"I'll take you home, Kate, as soon as I have a little talk with Nora," Patrick said, startling her.

But it looked as if Nora were having a talk with him. Kate couldn't help listening. "You keep talking like that, Patrick, and you'll find yourself fired and blacklisted. Not a mill in New England will hire you," she heard her say and would have followed to hear more if she hadn't been stopped by Patrick's mother, coughing.

"As soon as Pat takes you home, Kate, I want you to fix your hair. You and Clare take the children up to the church. I won't be going today. I'm going over to ask Maggie MacMahon to write a letter to Josephine about the new jobs here."

Kate didn't know how to reply. She didn't know who in the world Clare was. Or Josephine. Or Maggie Mac-Mahon.

"What's the matter with you today, Kate? You seem . . . so different."

Kate didn't know what to say. "I, um . . ."

"Well, just be sure you put your hair up. Perhaps Clare will help you. Imagine! Going to Mass with your hair down. I declare, sometimes you amaze me. Kate?"

"Mm?"

"Get your head out of the clouds and have some tea."

Kate stared at the kitchen. It was barely wide enough to hold a table. She looked at the large iron stove and tall black pump sticking up from the counter. She looked at the people. It was as if she were visiting a historical village, only these were real people, not guides in old-fashioned clothes. Occasionally one of them smiled and looked at her hair wonderingly, but no one, thank God, stopped to talk.

Kate stood dazed in front of the table, looking at the tea and scones. It gave her a small amount of comfort to know that scones were small biscuits with raisins in them. Her grandmother used to make them. But it wasn't comfort enough, she realized, as she picked up a blue teapot and heard the lid rattle. Her hand was shaking.

Embarrassed, she filled a cracked flowered teacup with

hot tea and set the pot down clumsily. She grabbed two scones, a cloth napkin, and her cup, and made her way through the small back hall that led off the kitchen to the backyard. Kicking the door open, she caught it with her backside so she could get through without having to ask anyone for help.

She sat down on a stone step and ate. The sun was higher. Birds sang. There was a pond to look at. Kate leaned back against the door, relieved that for a moment at least she didn't have to pretend she was anyone but herself.

She closed her eyes, but that proved to be a mistake. All the terrifying questions that she'd been holding off by her interest in the people and things around her came screaming back into her head. *Where is my mother? Where is my father? Where am I? How did I get here? When will I ever get home?*

As if she could run away from her fears, Kate jumped up and ran into the house. At the same time, unfortunately, Nora was coming out. They pushed at the door from opposite sides, then stopped and looked at each other. Nora stepped back gracefully and opened the door wide for Kate.

"Kate! 'Tis grand to see your hair so today." Her words floated toward Kate, and Kate was too dumbfounded to do anything about them. Nora waited. Finally, after an eternity, Kate managed to say, "Would ye like a scone?"

"No. No, thank you," Nora replied. "I'm afraid I'm too upset to eat just now."

"Well then, excuse me," said Kate. "If y' don't mind . . ."

Hennigan had said there wasn't very much food, but there seemed to be plenty, so Kate greedily poured herself another cup of tea and buttered two more scones. Whenever she was upset, she was hungry.

This time she ate standing by the table. Out of the corner of her eye she saw Nora waiting for her to come back outside, but Kate didn't want to talk to her again.

"Kate, 'tis time to go." Kate recognized Patrick's deep voice and her heart jumped. She jammed the last piece of scone in her mouth, swallowed her tea, and turned. His tall strong shape in the low doorway gave her a good feeling.

Following him out of the house, down the walk, and up the dirt road toward the O'Haras' house, she waited politely for him to speak, but he didn't. Kate guessed he was thinking about his poorly received ideas.

"Patrick," she said shyly, "y' spoke fine."

He sighed in exasperation but said nothing. Kate waited patiently. She watched her skirt and the toes of her shoes as she walked. All the women and girls had shoes just as ugly.

"I agreed with ye," she said, aware that her words were hardly spoken above a whisper yet unable to make them come out louder. She wanted to tell him she knew a little about strikes and unions and that in the years to come many people would feel as he did—and win too. But all she said was "I don't know what to say," which sounded peculiar.

" 'Deed, I don't know what to say either," he replied, unaware of her embarrassment. "Mick asked me if I was still going out with them tonight. 'The devil, Mick!' I said. 'Of course I'm going with you.' "

"Aye," said Kate, but what she wanted to ask was, What are you going to do?

As they turned the corner and saw the house, Kate hoped Patrick would be going in with her. Maybe she could somehow find out from him who Clare was. But she had no such luck. With a quick nod and simple "Bye now, Kate," he left her at the front path.

She hurried into the house and up to her room. No one else was there. Kate sat on her bed with her hands flat out on the quilt to steady herself. Perhaps if she lay down to sleep, she would awaken from the dream and be in the right place again.

Just as she lay down, the door to her bedroom burst open. It was the tired-looking girl. Kate jumped. She wasn't used to people barging in on her. She stared dumbfoundedly as the girl lay down next to her.

"What a bonny idea, Kate. We'll just go back to sleep." The girl shut her eyes, then opened them.

Kate stared.

"Ah, Kate, don't look so serious. I know we have to watch the children. I'm only having a joke with you." The girl got up and opened the trunk.

"Where's the comb?" she asked.

"I . . . I don't know," said Kate.

"Here it is," said the girl, smiling. "It fell to the bottom.

Now sit there on the edge of the bed and let me fix your hair proper."

Kate smiled back. So this was Clare. Kate and Clare were sisters. Not only that, they shared the same bed. As Clare brushed her hair, Kate stared at the other bed. Who in the world slept in that? Kate had a million questions and thought she would die if she didn't get them answered soon. Sitting there, having her hair brushed, she thought of telling Clare about herself but didn't. If she could convince anyone, it would have to be Patrick. He was the only one she felt at all connected to.

"Poor Ma," said Clare. "Do ye think she's getting worse, Kate? She coughed so much this morning."

"Aye," said Kate, not knowing what else to say.

"You do think she's worse?" Clare sighed. She pulled Kate's hair back firmly. "I do too. I tell you what. Let's go berry-picking down by the pond before we go up to help on the church. I wager Ma would like some fresh berries."

Clare gently tied a ribbon around the bun. "Done," she said simply.

Kate stood up and felt the lump of hair resting heavily on the back of her neck. She looked in the mirror and saw a more severe face on herself than she had ever seen. The center part was so rigid. All of her hair was pulled back so tightly, you couldn't even tell it was curly. It looked odd, but at least it was conforming.

"Thank y', Clare," she said.

Shortly after, Kate found herself and Clare picking currants and dropping them into little straw baskets along with Michael, a tousled, redheaded boy about nine, and Bridget, a sweet, blond, cherubic girl about six. They were on a bush-covered slope overlooking a pond behind the O'Haras' house. It was a beautiful day, and Kate found it surprisingly easy to fit in. The little kids were cute and they liked her. Kate spoke to them more than she had to anyone else, since they seemed the least likely to notice anything faltering about her accent. As she filled her basket, Kate was almost enjoying the pretense of being an old-fashioned Kate.

Perhaps the reason she felt so at ease was that the children didn't scare her. They were less serious than the grown-ups, though there was something about them that was a little strange. Occasionally they stopped to skip stones in the pond like regular, normal children, but as they walked around the berry bushes they talked about going to work at the mill. Kate didn't know if they were kidding or not.

As for Clare, Kate liked her except when she talked about Patrick and Nora, which she did incessantly, especially once they sat down in an open meadow for a rest. Wasn't Nora pretty? Wasn't her waist thin? Don't you think Patrick's lucky? Wouldn't it be grand if they got married next week?

There was something so simpy about Clare when she talked like this. She made Kate feel like showing off. In the middle of a long discourse on the beauty of Nora's hair, Kate could stand it no longer. She jumped up and did ten cartwheels in a row. When she finished, she threw

herself on the ground and looked straight at Clare as if
nothing unusual had happened.

Clare was shocked. "Who taught you that, Kate?" she
asked. Kate only smiled. Michael and Bridget were giggling as if Kate had done something indecent. "Y' better
not let Ma see you do that," Clare said, embarrassed,
but said nothing more about Nora.

There was something basically so sad about Clare that
Kate started to feel bad. Maybe it was her frailness,
maybe it was the circles under her eyes. She had been so
gentle with Kate's hair. Kate decided to be friendly again.

"Who's your favorite teacher, Clare?" she asked, roll-
ing over on the grass. It seemed a safe way to begin a
conversation with a girl she didn't know.

"Teacher?" Clare looked puzzled. "Why do y' ask? Y'
know there's no schoolmaster now. Ah, do y' mean that I
ever had?"

"Aye," said Kate, wondering if she should have started
this conversation.

"Well, there was Master Butler in Hartford, but I didn't
really like him. Did you?"

"Nae," said Kate. She couldn't think of anything else to
say on the subject that wouldn't give her ignorance away.

"If I ever leave the mills, Kate, I think I'd like to be a
schoolmistress. They're hiring some women these days,
I've heard. I'm sure I could be a better one than Master
Butler."

"Aye," said Kate.

"If only I could learn to read."

"Aye?"

"Ah, yes, Kate, I'd so love to learn to read! Why, then I could start teaching in only a few years!"

Kate held her head up on her hands and stared at Clare. She couldn't read? How old was she anyhow?

"If only the new agent would hire a teacher the way he's supposed to."

"Aye?"

"But I don't think he will. Mother's friend Mrs. Mac-Mahon says she'll teach me, but she's always too busy writing letters for everyone back to the old country."

I'll teach you, Kate wanted to say, but she held herself back. Someday, Clare, when Patrick believes the truth about me, I'll tell you too. And then, if I'm still here, I'll teach you to read, I promise.

But Kate knew she wouldn't be there for long and that Clare would probably never learn to read. Kate wondered again what year it was.

She lay back and looked at the clouds racing through the sky. Thank goodness, clouds are just the same everywhere, she thought. Any second now I could go back. I would blink and find myself lying in a lawn chair in my backyard, watching the clouds, and they would look just the same.

Suddenly it occurred to Kate how to find out how old Clare was and what year it was too.

"How old are you, Clare?" she asked.

"You know how old I am."

"I mean exactly how old in years and months."

"Well, let's see. Come back, Bridget, stay near us! Twelve years, and one, two, three months."

"Are you sure?"

"Of course I'm sure!"

"Well, let me check. I forget—when exactly where you born?"

"April, 1838. Why?"

Kate was too busy calculating to answer. Eighteen thirty-eight plus twelve is 1850. Oh, God! This was the year 1850!

Kate started to bite the inside of her mouth. It was a habit she'd been trying to get rid of and she had stopped it since New Year's, but this was too much. Her mouth was shaking, and if she didn't bite her cheek, she was afraid she would cry. How in the world did she get all the way back to 1850?

Little Bridget suddenly started to run back toward the house. "Come with me, come with me!" she begged as she was running. She ran across the meadow, spilling berries from her basket as she ran. The others laughed and followed, Kate stumbling after them. Bridget was running toward a shed in the backyard. There was a little shed just like it in back of every house on the street, Kate noticed. Outhouses, she realized. She also realized she needed to use one, and she did use it, aware in a terrifying way that her body didn't seem to care what year it was.

5

Soon afterward she, Clare, Bridget, and Michael were walking down the road to the church. They went the same way she had gone that morning with Patrick except that where they had turned right before, now they turned left onto a path. Ahead in a clearing was a new, small wooden church. On the roof was a short spire and on the spire two men were raising a wooden cross. One of them was Patrick. He had his jacket and shirt off. The muscles on his arms and shoulders bulged as he held the cross in place.

It doesn't seem right that he should think of me as his sister when I'm not, said Kate to herself.

There wasn't much work to be done at the church, but everyone who had been at the Mass was there and others had come too. People were enjoying themselves, eating, hanging around, cheering on those who were working. Some men stood with guns at the edges of the clearing. Michael and Bridget played tag with children their own age, and Kate and Clare helped some women transplant bushes and clumps of daisies into the soil banked up around the church. The greenery helped to relieve the newness of the church.

"Here, Kate, fetch that shovel over there and dig me a proper hole right here," said one of the women.

Kate obliged, glad to be of help at something she knew how to do. As she stuck the shovel into the ground, she suddenly noticed the numbers on the cornerstone. 1850, it said. It really was 1850! Kate raised the shovel and flung the dirt away from the church. 1850! This church is being built *before* the Civil War, thought Kate. These people don't even know that the Civil War is going to take place!

"Kate!"

She looked up. Patrick was standing on the corner of the roof just over her head.

"Watch out!" he yelled. Then he jumped down, landing like a cat on his feet. He grinned, proud of himself, and looked at Kate.

"Looks grand, doesn't it?" he said, giving her a big hug and looking up at the cross.

Oh, Patrick, thought Kate, feeling his arms around her. You make me feel so strange.

At supper he sat at one end of the kitchen table and Mother O'Hara sat at the opposite end. Along one side were Clare and Bridget; Michael and Kate were on the other. In the middle of the table were three bowls of steaming food: potatoes, stew, and cooked cabbage. The cabbage had the worst odor Kate had ever smelled. She had to breathe through her mouth so she wouldn't gag.

Patrick said grace. "Bless us, O Lord, for these Thy gifts, which we are about to receive from Thy bounty through Christ our Lord. Amen."

"Amen," echoed everyone, though Kate, as usual, was a little late in her response. During the prayer she had peeked at Patrick, expecting him to look up too, but his eyes stayed closed the whole time. She had never seen a boy pray like that.

Mother O'Hara shooed flies away with one hand and passed the cabbage with the other. Kate tried to refuse it, but Mother O'Hara said, "Take some," so kindly that Kate had to. She pretended to appear enthusiastic, but she truly didn't know how she was going to get the cabbage down. She tried mixing a little bit of it on her fork under a big piece of potato, but that didn't work. The way everyone was chewing so noisily made the cabbage worse than ever. Chewing and eating, passing and slurping—God, they were noisy eaters. Even Patrick. And there were flies everywhere.

" 'Twas a great mistake, saying that this morning, Pat," said his mother quietly.

Patrick turned red but he didn't reply.

"Y' know what happened to us when we first came. We couldn't find work and almost starved. We could have stayed in Ireland for that. At least now we've all got jobs."

Patrick looked miserable but kept on eating.

"Your father was a good man, God bless him. Sure he'd not like to look down and see ye siding with the Yankees."

Patrick slammed his fist on the table. "Why the devil can't anyone understand that I'm thinking of the Irish when I say we should turn out!"

"I'll not have you mention the Devil in this house, Pat!" shouted his mother, starting to cough.

"I'm sorry, Ma, I'm sorry," said Patrick genuinely. "I just—ah, never mind."

Everyone went back to eating without further word about the turnout.

"Eat your cabbage, Kate," said Mother O'Hara, finally catching her breath.

Kate tried but it was hopeless. With a sudden, anguishing pang of homesickness, she thought of her parents in the twentieth century, sitting on unpacked crates, perhaps in this very room, eating Kentucky Fried Chicken and talking about wallpaper.

Kate wondered if Patrick's sister Kate was sitting with them right now, gagging on the chicken. Kate wondered if her parents had noticed anything different about the other Kate, and guessed they probably hadn't. It made Kate feel awful to think they might not even be missing her.

"What are you staring at, Kate? I declare, you certainly are acting peculiar today." Mother O'Hara had stopped eating and was coughing with her mouth full. Any hopes Kate had of finishing her meal were completely dashed. "Get up now and help Clare with the dishes," Mother O'Hara said, wiping her mouth with the back of her hand.

Kate put Michael's empty plate on her full one and started clearing, but there was nowhere to clear to. No kitchen counter. No sink. Just a pump and a bucket. Kate stood there with the dishes in her hand, wondering what to do. She looked over at Patrick.

"Here," he said, clearing a space in front of himself and laying a towel on it. He set two big brown clay bowls on the towel.

"I'll help. I don't have to go out until later."

Kate frowned involuntarily. She was still standing there with the dishes.

"Don't worry, Kate. I'll be all right."

Clare brought over a tea kettle and poured boiling hot water into one of the large pottery bowls. Kate set the dishes back down on the table and stood by the hot bowl. She put her hand in the water. Yikes. It was so hot, she could hardly stand it, but she had at least figured out what was going on, and she knew she would rather wash the dishes than dry them since she didn't know where anything was stored. Patrick handed her a bowl with gray, gooey soap in it and a linen washcloth. He was humming as he dried the dishes. Listening to his deep voice, Kate was distracted from her predicament. She felt strangely contented just to be near him.

When the dishes were done, Kate and Clare sat on the front step and helped Mother O'Hara with her lacework until it got dark. She was working on a complicated pattern at one end while Clare and Kate added a border along the side she had already finished. Luckily crocheting was something Kate knew how to do, and by watching Clare, she caught on to the edgework quickly. The whole piece was about the size of a long narrow tablecloth.

Michael and Bridget chased fireflies as Kate and Clare made neat stitches around the lace. Patrick sat restlessly on the porch and didn't speak. He was waiting to find out when the boys and men were going out, Kate guessed. Finally he went inside and brought out a fiddle.

"This is a new song Mick taught me about a poor Irish lad who fell in love with the daughter of his British landlord. When the landlord found out, he bought passage for the boy's family and had them all shipped away to America." Though the tune he played was lively, there was something mournful about it. Maybe it was just the nervous feeling in the air. Kate wanted to ask what the men were going to do but she didn't dare.

A dark form moved up the road.

"Hennigan says ten, Patrick." It was James.

"Come, everyone, let's go up to bed now," said Mother O'Hara. "We've got all week to finish this, and we must be up early."

As the others went in and James went off, Kate leaned closer to Patrick. "I'll go with you and help, if ye want," she whispered.

"Don't be daft," he said out loud, getting up. "This is

men's work. You go to bed with the family." He leaned over and gave Kate a quick brotherly kiss on the cheek.

She hadn't seen any proper nightgowns in the trunk so she held back and watched the others undress first. Clare took off her dress, petticoats, pantaloons, and stockings but kept her slip on. So did the others. They folded their clothes and set them in the trunk. Apparently the slips were also nightgowns. Kate was relieved. She hadn't really relished the thought of getting completely undressed in front of the others.

Clare got into bed and talked in a monotonous sing-songy voice about Patrick and Nora again. Kate was glad when Mother O'Hara finally said, "Clare, you do go on so. If I were you, I'd say my rosary and go to sleep. We've had enough excitement for one day."

Kate got the brush out of the trunk and let her hair down. She brushed her hair as long as she could, postponing the moment when she would have to get into bed. She had never slept with another person.

"Ah, Kate, your hair was so surprising today," said Clare. "I thought you looked as beautiful as Nora." Wouldn't the girl ever shut up? Even though Kate had received a compliment, she was irritated.

"Thank you," she said though, trying to sound polite. After Clare fell asleep, *then* she would get in. Mother O'Hara and Bridget had said their rosaries and seemed to be asleep already in the next bed.

Kate knelt down and looked in the trunk again. She fussed around with the garments, rearranging them several times. She wondered where Patrick was. Mother O'Hara started to snore, Bridget was breathing heavily, but Clare wasn't asleep yet. God, Kate was beginning to feel so tired, she could hardly keep her eyes open. Rats, she finally said to herself, I'll just lie way over on my side so I don't touch her.

Kate's body and mind were so exhausted, she fell immediately into a sleep so deep that nothing in the world, past or present, could have awakened her except for the one thing that did: Patrick's hand on her shoulder. Kate opened her eyes and saw his silhouette in the moonlight.

"Kate, you've got to help me," he whispered.

"Of course, Patrick, what do you want?" Kate sat up, holding the covers in front of her. She remembered he had gone out at ten. "Are you all right?"

"Sh-h-h. I don't want to wake anyone. Come." He lit a candle next to her and in the yellow light she saw his dirty, sweaty face and a watery glare in his eyes.

"Patrick!"

"There's a terrible long splinter in my leg. Come."

Kate looked down at his leg. His pants were bloody.

They were ripped open all the way up to his thigh. Two inches up from his knee a jagged piece of wood was sticking out of his skin. A wave of nausea hit Kate, and looking away, she bit down hard on the inside of her cheek. She got up and followed him slowly into the bedroom he shared with Michael.

"Kate, you've got to pull it out without waking Michael." He sat on his bed, clenched his teeth, and spoke again. "It's not that deep, but it's got to come out right away." Patrick shifted his weight slightly and Kate could see how much pain he was in.

"All right, Patrick, tell me what to do." She willed herself to be competent and to do as he instructed. She tiptoed downstairs for towels, water, and soap. She went back downstairs and found a bottle of whiskey hidden under a floorboard where Patrick said it would be. She helped Patrick lie back as comfortably as he could on his bed, and putting towels under his leg, she did just as he said. With his knife she opened his trouser leg more, exposing his thigh almost all the way up to his crotch, but she couldn't think about that, couldn't look at the bulge in his pants up there, couldn't think about the strong smell of his body.

"How did this happen, Patrick?" she asked, carefully washing away the dirty blood that was matted in the thick hair on his leg. She willed herself to clean the area around the huge splinter. She could hardly see what she was doing, but she tried to be gentle. Each wipe made Patrick gasp.

"We set fire to Barlow's barn."

"Fire?" Kate couldn't believe that Patrick would actually do such a thing. "Ye set fire to a barn?" She brushed furiously at the flies that were circling over the gash.

"Well, we would have gone to the leader's house if we knew who he was. But Jamie Culkin, who went to Hartford at dawn for a delivery of whiskey, said he saw Barlow on the Hartford Road near where Father Tully was stoned, so we went to his house. Everything went fine until the last minute, when Barlow saw us and came out with a gun. He didn't hit any of us but"—Patrick stopped talking as she wiped directly on top of the wound—"but a shot exploded into a door near me as I ran by. It sent this piece of wood through my leg like a knife."

Kate could see the splinter clearly now. It pierced through the flesh on one side and stuck out the other. It must have been at least eight inches long. With a shudder she controlled a second wave of nausea.

"What do I do?"

Patrick handed her his knife. "Wash this well with hot water and soap. Then cut the skin above the splinter. Do it fast. Lift out the splinter and pour whiskey in the wound. But first, Kate, hand me the bottle."

Kate heard Patrick drink the whiskey as she washed the knife and dried it on a clean towel. She shut her eyes. "Please, God. Make me do this right," she said, and whether her words were silent or out loud, she didn't know. Nothing in her whole life had prepared her to do anything like this.

"Don't talk, Kate. Just do it. Now."

She walked over to Patrick without looking at his face. She looked at both ends of the splinter and slashed the skin from one end to the other. She had to press much harder than she thought. Had Patrick screamed? Michael turned over in his bed, then went back to sleep. She must have imagined the scream.

Numbing herself, she lifted up one end of the splinter. It didn't come free so she cut some more. Again she lifted the splinter, again she cut, and then at last it was out.

Without looking at Patrick's face, she put out her hand and grabbed the whiskey bottle from him. As she poured the whiskey on his leg, she heard a sob that wrenched her heart.

She folded a small cloth, soaked it with whiskey, and pressed it against the wound, making sure both sides of the cut were together. Carefully she wrapped bandages around the leg firmly but not too tight.

Neither Kate nor Patrick spoke. When she was finished, she looked at him for the first time since she had started. His eyes were closed and for an instant she thought of holding his head and shoulders in her arms and cradling them as he slept. Instead she put the bloody towels in a pile on the washstand and resigned herself to letting the flies settle there.

She cleaned Patrick's knife. The house was remarkably quiet. She could hear Mother O'Hara snoring from the next room, but that was the only noise. Kate sat on the floor next to Patrick's bed and laid her head against his mattress. She could feel the straw inside the ticking. Reaching up over the side of the bed, she found Patrick's hand and let her hand rest upon it.

Tears streamed down her face as she hoped this boy would be all right. He'd come to mean a lot to her. Way more, she realized, than Warren ever had. Warren. She couldn't even picture him in her mind. He'd never been a really serious boyfriend, though she liked him a lot.

"Kate."

He was awake.

"Kate, thank you."

"It's all right." She could hardly speak.

"You're a fine sister, Kate."

Kate wiped her face. She had to try again, even if he was hurt, even if he were to think she was crazy.

"Patrick," she said, trembling, "I'm not your sister."

He moved slightly in response to her words. "Ow!" He rested back again and lay still.

"Remember this afternoon when I said I was dreaming? Well, I was wrong, it wasn't a dream at all. You must listen to me because I could go back any time and I have important things to tell you. I'm from the future! And I think I've changed places with your sister."

Patrick moved his head and looked at her with pain and bewilderment in his eyes.

"Patrick, believe me! There's so much I could tell you about! Where I come from, we have cars that ride on paved roads, airplanes that fly in the sky, and spaceships that go to the moon!" She leaped up and pointed out the window just as the moon came out of the clouds.

Crossing back to Patrick's bed, she was startled to see his face. In the moonlight he looked gray, exhausted, and as old as her father.

"Kate, stop," he said wearily. "I don't need to be amused. I just need sleep."

"I'm not joking, Patrick, it's true," whispered Kate as she unfastened his other boot. "We have unions too." But he wasn't listening. This wasn't the time. She would have to wait. She lifted his shoulders and carefully took off his shirt. After shaking it as clean as possible, she folded it and laid it over the back of the chair. What about his trousers? She looked at them and realized, half with relief and half with disappointment, that they would rub the wound too much coming off.

Kate leaned over Patrick and pulled the covers up over his body, which didn't look so big now. Please, God, help his leg get well, and please, God, make him believe me next time.

As she left the room, Kate realized she had prayed more in that one day than she had ever prayed in her life.

7

She slept again, nightmarishly. Over and over she felt the knife blade in her hand. Over and over all night long she cut—slice, slice—through Patrick's leg and awoke to the rasping sound of his mother snoring.

When the early light of dawn finally appeared in the window, she opened her eyes slowly, half hoping to have returned home, half hoping to be still in the past. When she saw where she was, she started to cry. Squeezing her eyes shut, she turned over, trying not to awaken Clare. Slowly, slowly, she forced her breathing to be deep and steady enough so she could fall asleep one more time.

Suddenly a bell rang so loudly that Kate leaped out of bed. Clare, Bridget, and Mother O'Hara were getting up too. They all stood still for a moment, each of them dazed, taking a minute to adjust to the morning and a new day.

Finally Mother O'Hara started coughing, and everyone except Kate began washing up and getting dressed. The room was too crowded for Kate to move in so she sat down on the side of her bed. She'd always had a room of her own. She looked at the squares on her quilt and saw tiny hand-stitches.

"Kate!"

"Yes, ma'am?" Now where had she learned to say ma'am?

"Get dressed." Mercifully Mother O'Hara was leaving the room when she spoke. Clare left too. There was more room now.

Just as Kate was about to pull on her pantaloons, she heard Mother O'Hara and Patrick talking in the next room. Patrick's leg! She had forgotten! Kate yanked the brown dress over her head and ran into his room. Patrick was sitting up, showing his bandage to his mother, looking much better.

"It's just a scratch, really," he was saying.

"Show me, Pat," Mother O'Hara said.

"I can't. I don't want to take off the bandage yet. Maybe tonight."

"Can ye go to work?"

"I have to."

Kate was astonished. "Patrick, you can't go to work today," she said without thinking.

Her mother turned to look at Kate.

"What do you know about this?" she asked.

"She helped me put on the bandage last night," said Patrick. "When I came in, I asked her if she would help."

"I think y' better tell me," said his mother, turning to Patrick, "exactly what happened."

As Patrick told about the barn burning, Mother O'Hara didn't look happy, but she didn't look angry either. She rubbed her chin as he talked and every time he paused, she coughed and said, "God be with y'."

"A splinter stabbed into my skin. It was nothing, but we can't let the Yankees know about it or they'll burn our house. And I have to go to work today as if nothing happened. If the new agent sees me limping, he'll know it was me last night and he'll fire me for being a rabble-rouser. Lord have mercy, he could fire all of us."

Cough. "God be with y'."

Kate stared at Patrick. Yes, Lord have mercy and God be with you, she thought. I don't see how you're going to stand up.

"Kate, put on your apron and your petticoats. Help Bridget. Clare, you use the privy first. Pat, I'll help you get some clean pants on." Mother O'Hara's quiet determination set everyone in motion again.

"What time is it?" Kate asked, yawning.

"It must be four thirty," said Patrick, catching her yawn. He quickly pulled himself together. "Hurry now, everyone. The next bell will be at five and by then we better be through the mill gate."

"Work starts at five?" Kate was too astonished and tired to care what anyone thought of her unguarded question.

Patrick looked at her oddly. Just for a second she was sure he remembered what she had told him the night before. Then he laughed and said, "Aye, Kate, work starts at five. Now stop acting like a rich man's daughter and get going."

In less than fifteen minutes they were walking together down the street. Even the children. People came out of the other houses to join them. There were men, young women, a few older women, teen-agers, and children: at least fifty of them. It was like a parade, though the feeling was subdued, almost apprehensive. Michael ran ahead to see a boy about his own age, but Patrick called him back.

"Stay with us, Michael. In case anything happens."

It was amazing. Patrick was making himself walk as though nothing were wrong. Only once did he gasp, and that was when he heard Nora's call and turned back to greet her. She gave him a hug and wedged herself between Patrick and Kate in such a way that there was nothing Kate could do except move over.

Nora soon noticed something was wrong with Patrick. "What's the matter, Pat?" she asked, sounding alarmed.

But by that time they had turned the corner and were walking through a gate that led to several large brick buildings on the side of a river. The bell rang again, this time louder and five times.

"I'll tell you later," he said. "It's nothing. Don't say a word. Look how few workers there are this morning."

The bell was in a brick tower that rose up from the center of the largest building. A big black and gold sign beneath the bell said Lancaster Cotton Manufacturing Company. Two slightly smaller brick buildings were on each side. The early morning light made the brickwork rosy and the gold letters shiny. Narrowing her eyes, Kate stared at the buildings. They looked strangely familiar.

Once inside the gate, most of the workers stopped. They seemed unsure of where to go. Kate stared at the middle building. Somewhere—where? She was sure she had seen this place before.

Zing!

Zing! Zing!

Three shots rang out and sent the crowd, which had grown to about a hundred people, ducking and shrieking and running in all directions.

"Quick! In the main entrance!"

Everyone ran to the big door under the sign. It was awful because they all couldn't get in at the same time. People were shoving and shouting, children were crying. Patrick started to run in the direction of the shots, but Mother O'Hara caught his arm.

"Don't be a fool, Pat," she hissed. "Y' can't run! Stay here and let the others go."

The attempt to run must have sent waves of pain up

Patrick's body because he looked pale, as if he were going to pass out. Clare and Michael stood in front of Patrick so no one would see him limp. They're so calm, Kate said to herself. These kids are in the middle of a hysterical crowd that has been shot at, and they are so calm. She reached down and grabbed Bridget's hand. Some men with guns ran into the woods.

Fortunately no more shots were fired, and no one, miraculously, had been wounded. Kate managed to get through the main door with the crowd, entering a big room that looked like an old-fashioned bank.

8

"Good morning, everyone," said a tall, dour, gray-bearded man standing on a chair at the far end of the room. "I am glad to see that so many of you have come to work this morning. I am Mr. Harris, the new agent. Let me remind you, your houses and the general store are owned by the mill. I believe all of you owe money to the store. Should any of you decide not to work, therefore, you will be evicted and thrown in the almshouse until you can settle your debts. Are there any questions?"

The noisy, frightened crowd had quieted. Kate heard

bodies shifting and people catching their breath, but there were no questions.

"Very well." The tall man's voice was like ball bearings. His accent was English. Among all the Irish accents Kate had been hearing, his stood out, distinct, lofty, and cold.

"Now then, about that little unfortunate incident," Mr. Harris said. "I had several guards posted in the woods and around the factory this morning, so have no fear. The culprit will be apprehended within minutes. Now, I do not care who works for me, Yankees, Irish, Protestants, or Catholics, as long as they obey orders and cause no trouble.

"I am informed," Mr. Harris went on, "that there was an unfortunate incident of violence in this town last night." Kate felt Patrick stiffen, but she didn't look at him. No one did.

"I'm told you Irish like violence," said Mr. Harris, smiling condescendingly, "but remember, you may not carry arms. Do not take it upon yourselves to do the work of law and order. You will leave that to Mr. Lancaster, the constable, and me."

Kate felt the entire body of workers stir at his words. It was as if she could reach out and touch their loathing for this man. Yet everyone, even the youngest child, was silent.

"Now then," he said with a thinner version of his disgusting smile, "if, as I said, the Yankees don't want to work here, I do not care. This mill is being reorganized and I have jobs for anyone who can meet my terms and stay away from liquor. Is that clear?"

"Devil," whispered Patrick, but no one heard him except Kate.

"Good. Let's begin work. Mule spinners, if you had Yankee operatives helping you before, you may now select Irish ones to take their places."

People started talking and moving about. Patrick turned to Nora and Kate. "One of you can take Sandra Wolcott's place," he said.

"I will," said Nora right away.

Kate felt her heart stop. If she was separated from Patrick in this unfamiliar place, she wouldn't know what to do.

"Patrick," she said, grabbing his arm and trying to show with her eyes how serious she was, "please take me!" She was so desperate that she couldn't say anything more.

Fortunately Patrick seemed to get her message. He looked at Nora helplessly. "Well, if . . ."

Nora's eyes flashed. "I'll help you up the stairs," she said forcefully. "Come, children, let's go."

Kate squeezed Patrick's arm hard. "Patrick, please!"

"Why, I don't know, well, Nora, I . . ." Patrick looked bewildered.

"Stop fussing," said Mother O'Hara, looking at Kate. "What do you want to go with Patrick so much for?"

"She probably doesn't want to tend looms anymore," said Clare.

Bless Clare. Kate vowed to start teaching her to read as soon as she could.

"Aye. All right, Kate, you go with Patrick and the children. Nora and Clare, come with me to the weaving room."

Flushed with relief, Kate couldn't look at Nora, but she knew Nora was furious. Patrick led the way through a door and up a circular wooden stairway. He walked slowly and stiffly, up one flight, then into a long brick room with complicated wood and iron machines in rows that ran the entire length of the room. On both sides huge windows let in some light, and wall-mounted oil lamps provided the rest.

Letting himself limp now, Patrick walked up the aisle to the third machine on the left. It was a long machine with hundreds of threads going from the top down to a bar on the front.

"This one's mine, Kate," he said proudly, panting.

Uncle Mick walked over.

"How's your leg, Patrick?" he asked.

"Not too bad," said Patrick, and Kate realized how much it must have hurt him to walk up those stairs. He hadn't stopped to rest once.

"It was well worth it," he said to Mick with a chuckle. "Did y' hear? Did the barn burn down completely?" Kate looked around nervously to see if others were listening. Some of them were, but they all seemed friendly. She recognized many of them from the Mass and the church. The mood up here was completely different from the mood downstairs.

Suddenly, though, the workers stopped talking.

Patrick looked at Kate and spoke in a formal voice. "So, Kate," he said, "do y' understand how to piece on this machine?"

Out of the corner of her eye Kate saw Mr. Harris coming up the aisle.

God, she had never experienced anything like this: barn burning, gunshots, real people as enemies. The closest thing in her life was the annual basketball game between her school, Lancaster High, and North Catholic High School across town. Everyone cheered until they were wild and sick with excitement, and Kate had always felt that if Lancaster didn't win, she would die. But that was only during the game. Everyone knew the kids at Lancaster and North Catholic weren't really enemies.

But this was different. Mr. Harris was a real enemy and what she said now mattered. She could tell from the way Patrick was looking at her. Mr. Harris was almost to them.

"Could y' just go over it one more time?" she asked steadily.

Mr. Harris paused. He watched for a long time as Patrick explained the machine to her. Again Kate marveled at Patrick. You couldn't tell a thing was wrong with him.

Finally Mr. Harris walked on.

"Michael, fetch a basket of empty bobbins. Bridget, sit down and pay attention."

Michael walked over to the corner of the huge room and Bridget took a seat with a girl about her age in front of a nearby window. Kate wished she knew what she was supposed to do. She was standing to Patrick's left, about eight feet away. Mr. Harris walked back down the aisle to the stairwell. Everyone waited.

Then, with a monumental cacophony of cranking and slamming, the long iron rods over Kate's head started to

turn. Leather belts started going around. Wheels re-
volved. Various iron and wooden parts on the machines
started moving back and forth. The entire room was in
motion. The floor shook. The noise was overwhelming,
and Kate had to resist the urge to cover her ears with her
hands. It was like standing in an enormous barn filled
with running tractors, only there were no tractors, just
machines, and there was no smell of gasoline exhaust.

Kate was stunned. Before her were hundreds of threads
moving toward the bar that Patrick was slowly pushing
backward and forward. She stared at him. As he pushed
forward, his back muscles showed through his shirt. When
he pulled, he limped slightly. His leg must hurt terribly,
Kate thought. Was he okay? He was working so hard.

"Patrick," Kate shouted, moving close. "Can I help
you?"

"Quick! There's a broken thread. Tie it! And there's
another one over there! Hurry! Mr. Harris could be back
any minute!"

Kate ran to the first broken thread and tied the ends
together clumsily. Her fingers felt like hot dogs. She
reached for the other broken ends and tied them together.
She wondered if she was doing it right, but no one came
to check. Another thread broke, and they kept right on
breaking. Gradually she became used to the rhythm of the
machine. She would count to twenty, then a thread would
break. Sometimes she only got to ten. The job kept her
hopping. Her fingers loosened up.

"Bridget!" Patrick shouted.

Bridget ran around to the back of Kate's part of the spinning machine and, much to Kate's surprise, crawled under it and started to pick up tiny bits of cotton fluff from the floor and put them in a pocket in her apron. She reached up and pulled fluff off the threads too. All this she had to do when Patrick pulled the bar out. When he pushed it in, Bridget had to scoot backward like a crab and get out of the way. Kate hated to see her down there working so hard.

Michael brought over another basket of empty bobbins and set them down near Kate at the far end of the machine.

"I'll doff that full one for you," he said, pulling a full bobbin off the machine and instantly, it seemed to Kate, replacing it with one of the empty ones from his basket. Kate swept her eyes over her machine. There were several other full bobbins. She hadn't noticed them before. Apparently she was supposed to take them off and replace them with empty ones just as Michael had done.

"Would you doff the others for me too?" she asked, nonchalantly.

"Aye," he said, and as he did, she watched him closely. It wasn't hard, just a flick of the wrist here and a twist there and the full one popped out. The empty one went in just as easily. Kate saw a full one and tried it successfully.

For a moment she felt the kind of exhilaration she always felt whenever she tried something for the first time and found she could do it: the backhand stroke in tennis, a cannonball off the diving board. She could now work

the machine and keep up with Patrick. No one had noticed that she was a complete novice.

But her good feelings quickly disintegrated when she
looked down at Bridget, scuttling back and forth under
the machine. For an instant Kate was mad at Michael.
Why couldn't he do the dirty work? He's too big, she
realized instantly. She looked down the aisle.

Under every single spinning machine in the room was a
five- or six-year-old child picking up cotton. And they
didn't seem to mind. When they got their spaces cleaned
up, they crawled out backward and found their friends to
rest and play a bit. But after a while, back they went,
under the machines like little crabs.

Fifty knots later, Kate stopped noticing Bridget. She
was hungry and sick of tying, tying, tying. Her fingers
were numb. There were moments when she blanked,
couldn't remember how to make a knot, and had to talk
herself through it.

Take this thread in this hand and that thread in that
hand. Put this thread over that thread. Around and under.
Pull it through. Look for another broken thread. There it
is. Go.

She forgot about little Bridget underneath the threads.
She forgot about Michael carrying the baskets of bobbins.
Only the sight of Patrick kept her going. When she wasn't
tying threads, she watched him. He worked so hard. There
was a little wire he had to trip to make the threads fall at
the same time. He had to watch the bobbins and trip the
wire with his left hand at exactly the same time as he
pushed the bar with his right hand and nudged the car-

riage forward with his good leg. His work seemed very difficult to Kate, and she hated to think of his pain.

Once he looked over at her and smiled, but mostly he paid attention to his work, doing the same things over and over again. All the other men in the room worked the same way. There was no fooling around. A man came around and turned off all the lamps. There was enough outside light now to light the whole room.

God! She had never worked so hard. It was getting hot, and her nose itched from the increasing amount of cotton lint in the air. The work itself wasn't bad, but it was incessant, and her feet were aching. She was starving and her fingers were stiff. What time was it anyway? It must be almost lunchtime.

Just as she asked herself that question the bell rang again. Every machine in the room stopped. The floor ceased moving. The room was so quiet, Kate's ears rang. Patrick walked over and said, "Breakfast." Only breakfast! She felt she had worked all day. He leaned on her shoulder as they walked down the aisle. Mick came up and supported him on the other side.

"Are you sure you can make it, lad?" he asked.

"I've got to, Mick" was all Patrick could say.

Kate was hot and sticky, and Patrick was hot and sopping wet. His arm around her shoulder soaked right through her dress.

They walked down the stairwell. Patrick was leaning on Kate so hard, she thought she would fall over. She held on tightly to the banister.

"Where's Nora?" asked Uncle Mick.

"With Mother and Clare," gasped Patrick. "In the weaving room." But it was impossible for him to carry the discussion further. He was concentrating on getting down the stairs. On the way outside they passed Mr. Harris, and Kate could feel Patrick making an extra effort to walk normally.

The air was startlingly fresh compared to the dry, stifling air in the factory. The sky was blue with white puffy clouds floating in it. But nobody except Kate was looking at the sky and clouds. The rest were staring at a boy with straight blond hair who was chained to a tree in front of the factory. Kate was shocked. He reminded her of Warren, only he was a few years older.

"Stone him!" yelled Patrick.

"Throw him over the falls!"

"Tar and feather him!"

The boy looked terrified and furious at the same time.

"Stone him!" people chanted, pressing nearer.

"Nae!" shouted Kate, surprising everyone, herself most of all. She let go of Patrick and shoved to the front of the workers, pushing them back. She didn't know what had come over her except that she couldn't stand the thought of anyone hurting the boy.

"Nae!" she shouted again. Wildly she looked around to see if anyone felt the way she did. Not a soul spoke up. On the contrary even the children looked as though they would tear up the blond boy with their bare hands if they could.

She saw Mr. Harris coming over.

"Stop them!" Kate yelled, running up to him. "Or they'll surely kill him!"

Mr. Harris looked at Kate with disdain and walked over to the boy. The workers stepped back grudgingly to let him pass.

Mr. Harris folded his arms across his chest and said in a confident, stentorian voice, "Farther!"

The workers stepped back, but some were still shouting. Kate could hear Patrick's voice especially.

"Quiet!" yelled Mr. Harris. "That's enough! I'm not going to let a mob rule here. Now then, what is your name?"

"Jed Barlow," said the boy hatefully.

Barlow? Was this the Barlow whose barn was burned? The one who shot the splinter into Patrick's leg?

Mr. Harris walked over to Kate and stood right in front of her.

"What is your name, miss?"

"Kate . . . Kate O'Hara."

"Miss O'Hara," Mr. Harris said slowly, "I thank you kindly for your advice; however, I'm not in the custom of receiving advice from Irish mill girls."

Kate felt her face steam. His condescending manner made her feel embarrassed and furious. She felt like saying, You ignoramus, you think you're so hot and you don't even know the Civil War is coming. But she didn't say a thing.

Then Mr. Harris turned his patronizing sneer on the blond boy. "And you, Mr. Barlow, aren't you ashamed of yourself, shooting at these good, hardworking Irish people who have come to work this morning?"

"I know nothing about it," said Barlow defiantly.

"And who else was with you this morning?" asked Mr. Harris.

"I know nothing about it," said Barlow again.

"I see," said Mr. Harris. "So you're a Know-Nothing. Well, tell the others in your party, whoever the fools may be, not to bother me or my workers again." Mr. Harris didn't have to add, "Or there will be trouble," but Kate could tell he meant it and wasn't afraid.

Barlow looked as if he were going to spit in Mr. Harris's face, but something must have made him change his mind. Kate stared at the boy. It was hard to believe he was the one who had shot at Patrick last night. Right now he looked so furious, Kate thought he was going to burst into tears.

Mr. Harris spoke disdainfully to the workers. "I suggest all of you hurry home for breakfast now. Mr. Barlow, come with me."

Kate turned to Patrick, but he walked in disgust away from her and toward the gate with the other workers.

"What was that all about?" asked Mother O'Hara after she sat down at the kitchen table and started to eat. For breakfast there was cold oatmeal and milk. Kate couldn't eat. Everyone, especially Patrick, was mad at her.

"Aye?" asked Mother O'Hara.

"Oh, I don't know," said Kate, her eyes filling up. She hated to cry but she couldn't help it. She thought about

Barlow being led off to jail. She never should have tried to protect him. Tears ran steadily down her cheeks, but no one, not even Patrick, said anything to comfort her.

Finally Clare spoke. "I think I know what Kate was trying to do," she whispered. "She was trying to call attention away from Patrick."

The suggestion made so much sense that everyone immediately believed it. Once again Kate silently blessed Clare.

"I was thinking of doing something distracting myself," said Nora, who had come to the O'Haras' for breakfast too, but in their admiration for Kate no one paid any attention to her.

"You were wonderful," Patrick said later, back at work. "In all the excitement no one even noticed my bad leg."

The machines started up, filling the room once again with their deafening whirring and slamming noises. This time Kate moved fast. Though she hadn't eaten, she was filled with a new happy energy that came from people being proud of her.

I think I'll be all right here until I go home, she decided. Lucky things keep happening, and I think I know why. It's because I'm from the future. If something bad were to happen to me, I couldn't ever live in the future.

"Kate!"

"Yes?" She blinked.

"Get those loose threads! What's the matter with you! Hurry up!" Patrick was yelling at her and running his machine at the same time. He looked at her and then back at his machine and then back at her. Suddenly he tripped and put all of his weight on his bad leg.

"Jesus Christ and Mary!" he exploded.

Kate ran over.

"Are you all right?"

"Not unless you move faster, I'm not. Now for heaven's sake hurry and catch up with me. Mr. Harris could come by any minute!"

So Kate went back to tying knots, knots, knots. Her burst of energy faded and she moved like a machine. She worked for hours, and after a while the only thought that consoled her was the money she must be making.

Let's see, we started work at five this morning and it's almost noon. That's seven hours. Subtract a half an hour for breakfast, make it six and a half. Even if I'm only earning, let's say, a dollar an hour, I've made six dollars and fifty cents, and that will probably be worth even more when I go back because it will be antique money.

Kate's head started to spin as fast as bobbins on the machines. Say every dollar here will be worth ten dollars when I go back. Then I've earned sixty-five dollars so far today!

Kate didn't feel so tired anymore, but she *was* starving. At last the lunch bell rang. Food! Kate was so hungry that she didn't care what there was for lunch. She hurried home with the others and happily ate bread, cheese, cold potatoes, and berries.

Then she worked all afternoon. Hour after hour after

hour, Kate tied knots. She kept reminding herself how much money she was making. If she stayed a week and earned forty dollars, it would be worth four hundred dollars when she went back. Wow! She'd be able to buy a new pair of jeans, a jogging suit, a gray blazer, and maybe a chair for her parents. But the thrill of imagined purchases began to wear off as time passed and Kate felt exhaustion seep like poison through her fingers, legs, and feet.

She watched the sun drop lower and lower in the windows. At least at five o'clock she could go home and lie down on her bed. It was going to feel so good. She didn't care where she was or if a cow slept with her. That little straw bed was going to be heaven.

They walked home quietly and sat down to eat in their work clothes. Supper was cold ham, cold cooked cabbage, bread, butter, and tea. Kate ate it all.

Mother O'Hara and Clare talked discouragingly about the weaving room. Apparently each of the weavers had been given an extra loom to tend because there were so few workers. In consequence they were feeling exceptionally tired. Patrick looked grim as he heard the bad news but he didn't say what Kate knew he wanted to: I told you Mr. Harris would do that. Clare looked tired but bravely said her work went fine. As usual she talked about how wonderful Nora was. This time it was how clever and fast a weaver she was. Kate ignored her. She was too busy eating.

Patrick asked Kate to change his bandage, and she did

so by numbing her mind so she didn't recognize the red stuff as blood, the black lines as hairs, the purple areas as swellings, and the yellow bumps as dried pus. It was just a mixture of colors around which she was winding strips of cotton cloth. Gently, gently. Try not to make him gasp or else I will remember what it is that I am doing and throw up.

A hot bath. After this I will heat enough water to take a hot bath in a washtub and then I will go to bed. I don't even want to sit up and talk with Patrick. Nora can have him tonight.

"Thanks, Kate. Now clean up quickly and let's be going."

"Going?"

"Yes, going. Aye-yi-yi!" Patrick stood up on his newly bandaged leg. "Pass me the whiskey, Kate. I can't go back to work without something to cut the pain of this leg."

Back to work! Kate could hardly believe her ears. Back to work! She got the whiskey for Patrick and began to clean up. Her hands were so numb from tying knots, she could hardly pick up the old bandages and throw them out. Back to work! She couldn't imagine standing up for another moment.

10

For the fourth time in the day the factory bell rang. Kate thought the bell was inside her head, she had such a headache. Once again she, Patrick, Clare, Bridget, Michael, and Mother O'Hara walked to the factory.

Bridget and Michael were quiet. Kate looked at them. As she reached down and held Bridget's hand, the little girl looked up at her, smiling weakly. Poor Bridget. She was only six years old. She should be getting ready to go to bed. How could Mother O'Hara let her children work like this?

But in the crowd of workers gathering near the factory Kate saw other children Bridget's age. All quiet, all going back to work holding their mother's or father's hands. The whole crowd seemed quieter than they had earlier in the day.

"Wait!"

Nora ran over. Just when everyone was so exhausted, she would be running.

"How is your leg, Patrick?" she asked cheerfully. Once again she sneaked in between him and Kate.

"I'll make it," he said.

"You've been drinking!" she said. "You promised you wouldn't anymore! Didn't you hear the temperance speaker last week?"

"It hurts," he said sheepishly. Nora looked at him the way a mother would look at a two-year-old.

"Patrick," she said, "God be with y'. There are just two more hours to go. I'll come home with you tonight and help you change your bandages."

He didn't say, "You don't have to, Kate just did that." Instead, he looked at Nora gratefully. Kate couldn't stand to see them together, so without thinking she ran ahead. Patrick could get someone else to help him up the stairs. Panting, she reached the floor where the mule spinning machines were and found a short, plump, bald man she didn't recognize slowly walking around one of the machines.

He didn't seem to be one of the Irish. She felt embarrassed and noticed he seemed almost as embarrassed as she was.

"It's a beauty, isn't it?" he said finally, rubbing his hand on a wooden bar. "I'll hate to see it go."

"Go?"

"They've invented new machines that do this work even faster—miracle machines. But, you know," he said, "I love these old machines, even though they've been improved a hundred times since I started this mill." Why, he must be Mr. Lancaster, Kate realized. Others were entering the room. Patrick and Uncle Mick walked over. They looked shocked to see Kate and the mill owner talking together.

"Hello, sir," they muttered with extreme reticence and respect.

"Hello, lads," he said. "Glad to see you here today."

What was the matter with them? Kate wondered. Why did they act like puppy dogs? Just because this man was the owner? Just because he wasn't Irish? So what?

Mr. Harris entered the room. "To your machines!" he shouted. "Stop talking! Oh, I'm sorry!" He noticed Mr. Lancaster and walked right over. "Mr. Lancaster, sir, I didn't know you were here."

"Just checking on my machines, Mr. Harris."

"Of course, Mr. Lancaster. Come, let me show you the broadside I received today for the new Whitinsville machines."

Mr. Harris gave Kate a dirty look and took Mr. Lancaster by the elbow, steering him out of the room. Kate looked at Patrick watching them leave.

"Lord have mercy," she said. "What are you all so scared of him for?"

"He's the bloody owner," snapped Patrick. "Don't forget, he's the one who hired Mr. Harris and he's the one who last year cut your wages from three dollars to two dollars and seventy-five cents a week."

"Did you say two dollars and seventy-five cents *a week*?"

But suddenly all the machines in the room started up, and though Kate couldn't hear Patrick's answer, she could tell he hadn't been kidding. Kate inhaled the dust and oil in the room and gagged. Two dollars and seventy-five cents *a week*!

A thread broke and Kate tied it. Patrick yelled at Bridget and she scooted underneath. Michael carried a basket of full bobbins downstairs. Patrick pushed and pulled the bar of threads back and forth with concentration as the sun fell lower in the blue sky outside the vibrating windows. A man came around and lit the lamps again.

Kate hadn't known what tiredness was until now. It wasn't just in her fingers or legs, it was in her whole body. Her head ached so, she thought it would fall off. She had never in her whole life worked so long. Once she had walked to the other side of town with Warren, but that only took two hours. Before they moved she had cleaned her whole room, but that only took an afternoon. This was *all day*. Sure, they went home for breakfast, lunch, and supper, but all they had was a half hour for each and they had started work at five and weren't going to end until seven! A twelve-hour workday! And for what! She wasn't going to make it.

"Patrick!" she shouted.

"Aye?" He slowed the machine a little so he could look over.

"I'm too tired," she yelled, half whining like a baby but too exhausted to care. "I have to stop."

"Aye? No, it's okay," he yelled back. "If I stop, I'll never get started again. Better to keep going."

He thought she was inquiring about him. It made her feel guilty to be worrying about herself when his leg must hurt him so much. Okay, she thought. I'll do it. I'll stay right by him and finish if it's the last thing I do.

"Can I relieve you for a while, Miss O'Hara?"

It was Mr. Harris, being suspiciously polite. For Pete's sake, what did he want now?

"Have a seat," he commanded. "I have just heard from Mr. Lancaster that your brother is the best mule spinner in the mill. I'd like to take your place and try something."

"Do my job?" Kate glanced over at Patrick, who was looking as uneasy as everyone else in the room. They were continuing their work and staring at Kate at the same time.

"Yes," said Mr. Harris, and with that he reached over and tied a thread that broke right in front of the two of them. "I want to see how fast this machine can go. Go sit down."

Well, why not, said Kate to herself. Everything in my life is so crazy right now, I may as well take advantage of a little relief.

"If you say so, sir," she said and went and sat down on a bench by a window.

"You there!" Mr. Harris yelled at Bridget in the corner.

"Come over here and work." Bridget ran over and crawled under the machine.

Kate's heart ached for her. She looked so tired. But Mr. Harris wasn't tired. He tied knots the minute they broke, much faster than she did. Despite the animosity between him and Patrick they worked well together. Kate almost enjoyed watching them, both strong, both expertly trained for what they were doing.

"Faster, O'Hara," Mr. Harris shouted.

Patrick looked at him for a second in surprise, then began to make his machine speed up. He strained to push it in and pull it back as fast as he could. Kate knew his leg must be killing him.

"Faster!" Mr. Harris shouted fiendishly. He was practically jumping back and forth to get the knots that were now breaking at a much faster rate. He didn't miss one. Without being asked, Patrick moved the mule spinner even faster, as if he were trying to outdo Mr. Harris, to cause him finally to make a mistake. But nothing could stop Mr. Harris now. He was beaming horribly, Kate thought. She wondered whether Mr. Harris was trying to trick Patrick into revealing his wound, or if he really was just trying to see how fast the machine could be run.

Suddenly Bridget started to cry. She had been knocked over because the machine was going too fast for her. Patrick looked over at her and immediately lost his balance. With an agonizing short scream, he fell on his bad leg.

"Patrick!" Kate shouted, running over and kneeling down next to him. "Are you all right?"

"I'm fine," he said with his hand on his leg to cover what Kate knew was blood soaking through the bandage and his pants. "Just the Devil's luck, that's all." He glared at Kate in such a way that she knew she must stand up and act as if nothing much had happened.

"Come, Bridget," she said, getting up and dusting off the little girl's skirt. "You're all right now. Your machine's clean. Go sit on the bench. Michael, fetch that basket of full bobbins and take it downstairs."

Mr. Harris stood panting with his hands on his hips, looking down at Patrick. Kate and every other man, boy, woman, and girl in the room watched to see if he would start asking questions.

"You were very skillful on that machine," Kate said to Mr. Harris, intentionally trying to divert him. "I wouldn't have imagined it could go so fast."

Mr. Harris fell for it. "Yes, I told Mr. Lancaster these machines could be speeded up. This is our chance. With the Yankees gone and all their fool notions with them, I can speed up these machines and get this mill going so well, it will outproduce bobbin for bobbin every mill in New England."

Kate reached an arm down to Patrick but kept looking at Mr. Harris. "Aye, Mr. Harris," she said to keep him talking, "but what about the children? They can't keep up with that kind of pace." She felt Patrick slowly pull himself up.

"The children, yes, well, that can be solved, Miss O'Hara. Everything can be solved. We will use only the strong children. They will have to learn to work faster. It's just like hopscotch or any other game. They will have to practice."

"Perhaps, Mr. Harris," said Kate nonchalantly, but inside she was seething at the cavalier attitude this man had toward the children in his mill. Patrick was standing now, trying out his leg, walking without a limp to his position at the machine. With a clunk he engaged it, and Kate moved over to her position. She tied a knot, not daring to look over at Patrick for fear of crying out for him. Mr. Harris stood behind them and watched. Kate thought he would never go away, but finally he did. Even over the roar of the machinery, Kate swore she heard every worker in the room breathe a sigh of relief.

She looked at Patrick and saw him smile so gratefully at her that her heart soared. She almost wasn't tired anymore. They worked at a normal pace for about a half hour more, and then the last bell rang. Kate's first day at the mill was over.

11

Later at home she bit her cheek as she watched Nora help Patrick bathe his leg in a tub in the kitchen. She was exhausted but she didn't go to bed as the others had because when it came right down to it, she couldn't stand to leave Nora and Patrick alone.

She didn't know how long she was going to be back in the past, but looking at Patrick with Nora, she knew she was going to try again soon to convince him he was not her brother. If by chance she was going to have to stay here for a long time, it would be impossible to sit back and watch them together like this.

"Careful, Nora!" Patrick shouted.

"Of course, darling," said Nora. Nora dabbed at the wound with a damp cloth, trying to clean off some of the dried blood around the edges.

Kate thought it would be better just to leave the wound as it was. After all, what was the sense of cleaning it on the outside if it hurt Patrick? The danger was germs inside. "Why don't you pour some more whiskey on it, Nora? That will kill the germs," said Kate.

"Kate, dear, I've done this sort of thing before. I think I know what I'm doing."

"But water won't help, Nora. You're just pushing the germs around."

Nora finally rose to the bait. "What are germs?" she asked.

Kate almost laughed. "Bacteria," she said.

Nora made an exasperated *tsk* noise with her tongue.

Kate got up and walked over to the window and looked outside. The only thing she had that Nora didn't was knowledge. But she had to be careful. She couldn't flaunt it too much without giving herself away. Nora would probably be only too delighted to discover Kate had "brain fever."

Nora stood up and got the whiskey bottle from the kitchen shelf. She poured some whiskey on Patrick's leg and he screamed.

"That's too much!" Kate yelled. "Oh, Nora, you should have let me do it!"

Nora threw the rag down on the floor and stood up.

She looked at Kate and then at Patrick as if she was going to cry. Instead, with a toss of her head, she walked out of the house and slammed the door behind her.

Kate looked at Patrick. His eyes were closed.

"Patrick!" she said, putting her hand around his shoulder. "I'll bandage it and help you up to bed so you can lie down."

She was never so gentle as she was now, partly for Patrick's sake and partly, she had to admit, to prove that she was better at this than Nora.

"Kate, what did you do that for?" Patrick finally said.

"Do what?"

"Be saucy like that to Nora."

"I just wanted your leg to heal, Patrick," said Kate, tying up the bandage. She lifted Patrick's arm and helped him limp up the stairs.

"You don't like her, do you?" he asked after he lay down. "Neither does Ma, I sometimes think."

Kate sighed. She looked at Patrick's tired face and didn't know what to say. Maybe this was her chance. Maybe not.

"Oh, she's a good enough lass, I suppose," she said, and then changing the subject, "Do you need anything?"

"No, no, thank you."

Kate helped Patrick take his shirt off and get his legs under the covers. He didn't say a word about taking off his pants. Apparently it didn't bother him to sleep in his clothes.

"Do . . . do y' love her, Patrick?"

It was a bold question, but since he thought she was his sister, she could get away with it. Kate sat on the edge of the bed and looked at the wide-planked wooden floor. She wondered how she would feel if he said yes.

"Ah, Kate, sometimes I swear I don't know."

Kate's heart turned around inside her.

"Sometimes I think she's the most wonderful, most beautiful girl I ever met, Kate. I think to marry a girl like that would surely be a wondrous thing."

Her heart slid down into her stomach.

"But other times, like at the Mass yesterday, I feel she's different from me. She doesn't understand the way I think. Nobody does."

I do, Kate wanted to say.

"I don't know, Kate, sometimes I feel as if I'm from a different world. A world even farther away than Ireland."

Of all things to say, this was too much. Kate shifted her position on the bed and got ready to tell him again.

"Patrick," she said, trying to keep her voice calm and steady, "do you remember what I told you last night?"

"Aye?"

Kate swallowed. "About how I'm not really your sister. About how I come from the future. That's how I know about germs and unions and cars and spaceships and frozen pizza and records and—"

The look on his face stopped her. She could tell he didn't believe a word she was saying. He seemed to be thinking, Oh, Jesus and Mary, not again. It's bad enough with the turnout and the mill and Mother's cough and trying to get along with Nora.

"Patrick, really!" She grabbed his hands. "You've got to believe me. I know you have a sister named Kate, but I'm really not her!"

"Kate." He held her hand firmly, settling back against the pillows so he could be comfortable enough to hold her hand and talk to her. His blue eyes stared at her. "Kate. What in heaven's name is the matter with you?"

"Patrick, listen. I know it sounds crazy, but I swear it's true! Where I come from, it's more than a hundred and thirty years into the future. Things have changed! People don't work twelve hours a day in mills. My father works in an office from ten in the morning to six at night. He has an hour and a half off for lunch. He goes to fancy restaurants for lunch." She had dropped her accent and was racing now, trying to pile up enough details to convince him. "All different ones. Sometimes he even lets me come with him. My favorite one is called Le Factory. It's in this grand old building and the food is French . . ." and, oh, God, she was talking so fast, it almost slipped by her. Le Factory came into focus as if her mind were a slide projector. Along came another slide, the Lancaster Cotton Mill. A double exposure with no confusion. The two buildings were the same. The building she had worked in all day was the same building that had been fixed up as part of her town's historic renewal. Her mother had been on the committee. The factory had been converted into a chic French restaurant.

"What's the matter, Kate?" Patrick asked, concerned by the look on her face. "Why are you talking that funny way?"

"Oh, Patrick, you wouldn't believe it, you just wouldn't believe it—where I come from the Lancaster Cotton Mill is a French restaurant." She started to laugh.

"French restaurant? What's that?"

"Oh, Patrick, this is impossible!" And it was. She couldn't stop laughing. She held her stomach and laughed and laughed and laughed until tears streamed down her cheeks. Suddenly her shoulders began to shake and she was sobbing.

Patrick pulled her over against his chest and put his arm around her. She cried steadily. At first Kate was so relieved to be comforted that she didn't feel his skin, but then as her sobs subsided, she felt the muscles of his arm moving rhythmically as he stroked her head. She felt the wetness of her tears against the hair on his bare chest and, without thinking, put her hand up to curl some of it in her fingers. Patrick abruptly tensed and pushed her away. In an awkward, breaking voice he whispered, "Lord Almighty, Kate, what do y' take me for? You're my sister."

Kate lifted her head. He looked guilty, and she knew why. For an instant she had felt him respond to her.

Kate stood up. She couldn't stand the guilty look on Patrick's face. It made her feel awful! She *must* make him believe she was not his sister; otherwise he would think she was a pervert. She started to tell him again but lost the opportunity as the door burst open. It was Mother O'Hara.

"What are you doing up, Kate? You look so tired."

"Just helping Patrick."

"Have you been crying?"

"Aye. A bit. I guess I am tired."

"Well, you did a good job helping him. Now go to bed. Before you know it, the four-thirty bell will be ringing."

As Kate closed the door she heard Mother O'Hara ask Patrick, "What happened to Nora, Pat? I passed her on my way back from Maggie's and she looked madder than a tricked leprechaun."

"I don't know. Something Kate said to her about the way she was fixing my leg."

"Hm-m-m. Well, your girl friend seems a little high-strung to me. Here, look at me lace. How do you think your father would have liked it? God Almighty rest his soul." Mother O'Hara started to cough.

"How are you feeling, Ma?"

That was all Kate heard. She crawled into bed next to Clare and fell asleep.

12

The next morning Patrick avoided her. He left ahead of the others to go to work, and when she arrived, he didn't even look at her. When he had to speak to her, he did so politely, but it was as if he were speaking to a leper. Kate knew he was afraid of what had happened the night before, and she knew she had to talk with him again, but every time she tried to say even a word to him, she was rebuffed.

"How's your leg, Patrick?" she asked as they walked downstairs for breakfast.

He pretended not to hear and started up a conversation with Uncle Mick instead.

"Would you like another piece of my cheese?" she asked at lunch. But he shook his head and asked Michael to pass him the lemonade.

Kate felt her face burn. "You idiot!" she wanted to scream. "I'm not your sister! You don't have to treat me like this!"

Every time she came near him, it seemed, he was talking about Sunday, the first time the new church would be used. It was, besides the turnout, the big topic of the week, and Patrick threw himself into it. Kate had never heard him ask Nora's opinion about anything before, but now, whenever Nora, Patrick, and Kate were together, he made a point of asking Nora what she thought about everything. She said she didn't believe there would be any more trouble with the Know-Nothings. They had stoned the priest and shot at the crowd. Sure, the Irish had retaliated once, but since they hadn't retaliated for the shooting, the Yankees would calm down. After all, America was supposed to be a country of religious freedom.

"Y' don't understand, Nora," said Patrick patiently. "We *have* retaliated. We've taken their jobs. Sure, Jed Barlow will be let go by the constable; after all, he's a Yankee too. But you know Jed's father. He and the other Know-Nothings are fuming. If they hear about the church opening Sunday, they'll be there for sure."

"Trust in God," said Mother O'Hara, coughing.

"Aye, and guard the church at the same time," said

Patrick. "I tell ye, it's a shame we didn't turn out with them. We might have gained their trust and gradually their tolerance."

"Ah, now, don't be starting that again, Pat," said Nora.

"But—but he's right!" stammered Kate boldly. Maybe she could win Patrick back this way. "If we had supported the demands the Yankees were making, Mr. Harris would have had no choice but to grant them. And then the Yankees would have accepted us. Lord Almighty, who knows? Someday the Irish and the Yankees may live in peace together and not even care who's what." Kate looked over at Patrick, but he looked disgusted.

"I'm sure," he said to her sarcastically, "the Irish and the Yankees will always know the difference between them." He got up. "Come, Nora, let's be going back." He pulled her up by the hand and left Kate sitting behind.

Days passed, and Kate became more and more anguished. Every time Patrick was with Kate, he was antagonistic. Every time he was with Nora, he lavished attention on her. Kate was mad, but she was not a fool. The very extent of Patrick's efforts to demonstrate his affection for Nora convinced Kate he had felt something for her. Finally she decided to ignore him for a few days, to let things cool off. Then, when he had relaxed a little, she would try again.

All week long she worked as steadfastly as she could at the mill. It was monotonous but at least she was gaining skill and strength. Each night she was exhausted, but the thought that eventually she would make Patrick understand kept her preoccupied. The work week was six days long and by Saturday Kate was fed up by everything. She'd waited long enough. She would talk to Patrick that evening no matter what. Sunday was the opening of the church, and she wanted to be able to go there with him as friends.

After work she went home and stepped out into the backyard. She sat on the back porch and waited. Sooner or later he would have to come and use the outhouse. There! There he was! She waited. A few minutes later he walked back to the house.

"Patrick," she called from the shadow of the house.

"Who's that?" he asked, startled.

"It's me—Kate. Please. Don't go away."

"Now what do y' want?"

"I just want to say I'm sorry."

"Aye?"

"Please listen. I'm not insane."

He was standing awkwardly in front of the back door.

"I'm scared, Patrick," she said, stepping forward. "I don't know what is going on and I'm afraid. You're the only one I trust to help me."

"Y' mustn't think of me that way!" said Patrick fiercely. "I—I've got to hurry to the church. I've guard duty there." He opened the door, entered the house, and slammed the door in Kate's face.

Kate couldn't go in. She walked around to the front of the house and watched him hurry down the street. Slowly she walked the opposite way to the mill. In the darkness she couldn't tell if the sign said "Le Factory" or "The Lancaster Cotton Manufacturing Company." I give up, thought Kate. I'm going home.

She walked back to the O'Haras' house resolutely. I came here through sleep, I'll go back through sleep, she said, feeling a bit better. On the front porch Mother O'Hara was finishing her lacework by candlelight. "I thought I'd do a panel of your father and the baby Jesus sitting together in Heaven, Kate. What do ye think of that? 'Tis a grand idea, aye? I don't care if it takes me all night to finish. Tomorrow when I go to church, your father will be there."

But Kate didn't want to talk. "Bye," she whispered sadly as she let herself in the front door. She meant it. She was never going to see Mother O'Hara again.

Kate undressed and got into bed. Clare and Bridget were already sleeping. Good-bye, Clare. Bridget. Michael. Patrick. Kate pictured Patrick standing tall and straight on the church steps. She wished she could see him one more time. Oh, what difference did it make?

She closed her eyes and concentrated on going home. She thought about playing Scrabble with her father. She thought about her friends coming home from camp and asking her what she had done that summer. They'll never believe it, she said to herself.

Until now she had been sure that if she really wanted to leave, she could. That first day, when she had tried to pinch herself back into the future, it hadn't worked because a part of her was curious enough to want to stay and find out more.

But now she knew all she wanted to know. She had met Patrick and he didn't like her. She had seen the nineteenth century and was sick of factory work, potatoes, outhouses, and flies.

Kate lay in bed, psyching herself up for the return trip. On the first day of school she would wear jeans and a new red blouse. She might start wearing her hair differently. She would probably like English better than history this year. God knows, she'd had enough history to last her a lifetime.

She thought about her room and wondered if she should push her bed all the way over to the wall and make a daybed out of it. She could get a new cover, dark blue or yellow. She thought about her records and she thought about Warren. After Patrick it was going to be a disappointment to see him. Well, she couldn't help it. She was going home anyway. Eighteen fifty is a real drag, she said to herself. There's no TV, no record players, no dishwashers, no toilets, no hot showers, no Tampax. Clare had just started her period and Kate had watched with dismay as Mother O'Hara took some rags out of her trunk and told Clare to tie them around her and wash them out at night. Kate was aghast. She would certainly be glad to get home before she got hers this month.

Kate heard Clare sigh and, despite her sympathy for the girl, felt like kicking her. She tried to hate everyone and everything about the year 1850. She certainly hated Patrick. She hated sharing a bed, hated to see children in a factory, hated to work so hard, hated horse manure in the road.

In spite of her fury, though, pleasant but uninvited thoughts kept popping into her mind. The trees and the fields, the clear water in the mill pond, the pretty long dresses, Patrick. No! She didn't like Patrick. Not at all! She wanted to go home *right now*!

Kate waited for a long time, then pinched herself all over harder and harder. Nothing happened. She waited and felt her stomach cramp. She dug her fingernails so hard into her palms that she almost drew blood. She bit the inside of her cheeks and tasted blood, but still nothing happened.

Suddenly she knew for certain what she hadn't been able to face before. She was never going back. She was stuck in the past forever. Kate turned and sobbed into the lumpy straw mattress. She wanted to tear it and rip it into shreds and throw it around the room. She wanted to push Clare out of bed and stuff straw down Bridget's sweet-breathing throat.

Mommy! Daddy! Why can't you help me?

She leaped out of bed and ran downstairs. She flung open the front door and stood panting on the front porch.

"Begor, Kate, what ails ye, lass?" It was Mother O'Hara. Kate had forgotten all about her.

"'Tisn't decent standing there like that. Here, put this on." Mother O'Hara handed her a shawl. Kate wrapped it around her shoulders and pulled it tight.

"There now, child. Have a seat. Y' can keep me company."

Kate sat down and shivered. She heard crickets and someone down the road laughing drunkenly. She heard

Mother O'Hara's raspy, labored breath and suddenly felt as sorry for her as she felt for herself.

Mother O'Hara worked on her lace with an energy that amazed Kate. Her fingers never stopped moving unless she had to cough. She would begin at first with a small catch in her throat, and then if she couldn't conquer it with a quick, efficient hack, she would resign herself to go on coughing wearily for a full minute. Eventually the cough seemed to go away, not because it had cleared up her lungs, but because she wasn't strong enough to go on.

Mother O'Hara coughed all day at the mill and half the night in bed. Her cough was a part of her, and it had never struck Kate one way or the other until now, when she was sitting so quiet and so close. If I am here for good, Kate thought starkly, then Mother O'Hara is really my mother.

She pulled the shawl around her so only her bare feet stuck out into the cool night air, put down her head, and wept.

"There, there, Kate. If ye think ye've got it bad, think of your poor father dying on shipboard. Think of Margaret still scratching potatoes out of the soil in Ireland."

Kate listened and rocked to the gentle rhythm of Mother O'Hara's words.

"He was a good man, a fine man, your poor father, may the Almighty God bless him and keep him and watch over him. 'Tis a shame he can't be here tomorrow to see the church, Kate, but look here at the lace. Surely it's the grandest thing I ever made. See? Right here, there's your father and the Christ Child."

Kate lifted her head out of the shawl. In the candlelight the lace was textured, airy, and white. It was incredibly complex, and sure enough, there at one end was a faint picture of a man holding a baby in his arms.

"It's grand," Kate said sincerely.

"Father Tully will be pleased, don't y' think? Even if I have to stay up all night, it will be finished by morn."

"I'll help you," said Kate quietly.

"Why, that's a fine lass. Bless you. This section here needs fringe."

Kate took the silk thread she was given and started on the fringe. The work calmed her. All was quiet save the crickets and Mother O'Hara's breathing, which seemed easier now.

A train whistle blew. "The midnight train to Boston," said Mother O'Hara. "I wake up every night when it goes by. Mind you, we've six hours until Father Tully comes. I'd surely like this to be in the church when he arrives."

All night long they worked. At one point Mother O'Hara taught Kate a more complicated stitch, and when she picked it up quickly, she could tell Mother O'Hara was proud of her.

If I can't go home and Mother O'Hara is my mother, then I must accept Patrick as my brother, thought Kate. But when he returned from guard duty, Kate couldn't look up.

"Good night, Ma," he said.

"Night, Pat," Mother O'Hara answered softly.

He didn't say anything to Kate, nor she to him, but as she heard the door shut she couldn't help sighing.

"Kate?"

"Aye?"

"Look at me."

Kate looked up at Mother O'Hara. It seemed now even the crickets had gone to sleep, it was so quiet. Dawn had not begun, yet the darkest time of night had passed, and Kate could see Mother O'Hara's tired face clearly.

"What is it?" asked Kate.

"Ah, I don't know. Just something I was feeling. Never ye mind."

Kate went back to her work.

"For sure, it's a queer world," Mother O'Hara said.

Kate wondered what she had been about to say. Maybe she was thinking about the new church. Maybe she was missing her husband, wishing he were alive to see it.

At last they finished the lacework and Mother O'Hara stood up. "Let's take it to the church now, Kate," she said excitedly.

It seemed like a good idea. Kate had long since given up any hope of sleeping, and it would be pleasant to walk through the streets at dawn with Mother O'Hara feeling so proud of her lace.

They folded the altar cloth carefully, and Mother O'Hara carried it. As they walked slowly down the street Kate was suddenly certain that she would never forget the dark pink-gray color of the night, the stones that lay in a ridge along the middle of the road, and the song of a single bird up earlier than his comrades.

She and Mother O'Hara didn't speak. It wasn't necessary. Her real mother would have said, "Is something troubling you, dear, that you want to tell me about?" Kate didn't always feel like discussing her thoughts.

"Who's there?"

It was James, standing at the edge of the church clearing.

"It's Kate and me," said Mother O'Hara. "Have no fear."

"What are y' doing here?"

"We came to put the altar cloth on the altar. Look, James." Mother O'Hara gave one end to Kate to hold and unfolded the other end for James to see.

"Ah, that's lovely now," he said. And it was. It seemed to collect and reflect all the predawn light that was in the air. "Say, if you are here, would y' mind if I left for a minute? There's been some confusion. Mike MacMahon was supposed to have relieved me an hour ago, but he hasn't shown up. I'd like to fetch him."

"Aye, run along, James. There, Kate, take his rifle."

James handed over his gun to Kate. It was long, awkward, and very heavy in her hands. "Come back soon," she said, wanting to add, "because I'd never use this on anyone."

James ran down the path. Mother O'Hara pushed open the door of the church and they entered. "God bless," murmured Mother O'Hara, crossing herself and kneeling. Kate copied awkwardly, the gun hitting her knees.

Together they walked up the center aisle. The colors in the stained-glass windows were peaceful and muted because of the early dawn light, and Kate was surprised to find herself looking forward to seeing them later with strong sunlight pouring through.

She had arrived a week ago, she suddenly realized. The Mass at Uncle Mick's house was only last Sunday. It felt much longer.

At the front of the church they placed the lace on a special wooden table with an inlaid marble top. The lace hung down four inches on each side. It was perfect. Kate felt proud of the section she had done, and as Mother O'Hara gazed tearfully at the picture of her husband and baby Jesus, Kate was moved to put an arm around her.

It would be best to accept the fact that this woman was her mother, that Patrick was her brother, and that she should never again say anything to him or anyone else about having come from the future. Kate heard MacMahon come up the church steps. Maybe she could find another boy to like. Maybe James. No, Patrick was the only one she had met who . . .

She looked toward the door and thought she saw Warren. Oh, my God. Not Warren. It was Jed Barlow with two older men behind him.

"Put up your hands," one of the men said. They had guns and sacks. "Put up your hands, I said!"

Mother O'Hara gasped and started to cough. Kate put her hands up and looked for her gun. Where had she set it down? There it was, on the front pew, too far to reach. What a stupid place to have put it! She glanced at Mother

O'Hara, who was looking at the gun too. Her arms were up in the air, bobbing up and down because of her coughing.

Jed Barlow stayed by the door. The other two men were walking down the aisle. Irrationally yet instinctively, Kate and Mother O'Hara moved to the front of the altar, protecting the lace from their sight.

It was hard for Kate to be afraid of Jed because he looked so much like Warren, but she could tell by Mother O'Hara's trembling that just now fear was sensible. The other men *were* frightening and they were coming closer.

They stopped at the front pew and glared. One of them said, "What are you two Paddy lassies doing here? Are your men too afraid to guard their own church?"

Kate hoped they wouldn't see the gun. She didn't know if she could fire it, but maybe Mother O'Hara could.

One of the men swung his bag down on the pew. It landed with a sharp clatter on the gun.

"I see you've made me a present," he said, picking up the gun and hefting it. He aimed at them. "What are you hiding behind you? Move aside!"

They moved, leaving the altar exposed. He stared at it, confused.

"It's me altar cloth," said Mother O'Hara. "I just finished it. Please don't harm it."

"Altar cloth!" The man snatched the cloth off the altar and let it fall to the ground. "We don't want Papists in Lancaster!" he shouted. He fished around in his bag and took out some straws and a flint. Kate gasped as he struck the flint and lit the end of one of the straws.

"You think because they put my son Jed in jail for a few days we'd change our minds about Irish Catholics? We are *free* men here. We bow to no king and no pope. It's bad enough that you took our jobs. Did the Pope tell you to do that? Is that part of his plan?"

Jed's father started toward the altar cloth as Mother O'Hara screamed out "Nae" and started to weep. Desperately Kate said, "Please, can't you leave that? If you have to burn the church down, for God's sake please start somewhere else."

She thought if the men went over to a corner she might be able to run to the gun, but no, though Jed's father turned away from the cloth, he took both guns with him and he was watching her constantly.

At first there was just the smell of smoke and the steady sound of Mother O'Hara's weeping. Kate kept hoping MacMahon would return. When he came in the door, she would run at Jed. Maybe she could grab his gun and use him as a hostage the way she'd seen people do on TV. She repeated over and over to herself the logic she had worked out about not being able to be killed, because if she were, how could she live in the future? It didn't seem so logical now. She could be killed now, go to Heaven, and be born again at a later time. A sick, acid taste came into her mouth.

At the back of the church Jed Barlow was laughing. "When this church is destroyed, maybe you Irish pigs will get the idea that we don't want foreigners around here."

Smoke was coming from about five places in the room now, and Jed seemed delighted. He walked down the aisle and kicked the altar cloth with his dirty boot. Mother O'Hara bowed her head, sobbed, and coughed.

When was MacMahon coming? Couldn't he see the smoke from outside? Why didn't he warn the others? Perhaps he already had. Please, God. Please, Patrick; please, everybody, help us, Kate prayed.

"All right, go," sneered Jed. "By the time you get help, it will be too late." He laughed. "We're not going to kill you." Jed smiled the smile of the righteous. "We just don't want your church here."

One of the older men added, "And we don't want you to say who you saw here. If you do, I or someone else will come after you. No, not you, the two little ones. What are their names? Michael and Bridget? Never mind, we know who they are and where you live: halfway down Paddy Lane, ain't that right?"

"You bastards!" Kate yelled in spite of herself. "You rotten bastards! You think by starting a fire in this small church, you can keep Catholics out of Connecticut! Why, you're as stupid as the Ku Klux Klan in the South. Only instead of hating blacks, you hate Catholics!"

He was staring at her, eyes wide open, pointing the gun right at her, but he seemed too stunned to shout. In her rage, she suddenly realized, she had unwittingly dropped her Irish accent. Still, she couldn't stop herself.

"You jackass!" she cried. "Catholics don't take orders

from the Pope! They're just as good Americans as you are! Oh!" She noticed that the smoke had little orange flames licking up in it and that the air was thick.

Mother O'Hara coughed continuously now, her body heaving and trembling in Kate's arms. Kate put her head on Mother O'Hara's head and sobbed.

The men were staring transfixed at Kate. Jed Barlow walked back and forth angrily and started to say something a few times, but he never did. He seemed anxious to get out of there.

The flames were getting bigger. The room was getting hot.

Finally he said, "Come on, Father. Let's get out of here!"

"But just remember," one of the men shouted back, "you don't know who set the fire!"

Kate wanted to run out of the church as fast as possible, but she couldn't. She had to help Mother O'Hara, who could hardly walk. It took an eternity, a hot, smoky, hellish eternity to help her down the aisle. Kate looked back only once. The men were nowhere to be seen. They must have slipped out the back door.

At last she reached the door, opened it, and staggered out into the fresh air. Kate immediately started to scream, "Fire! Fire!" She dragged Mother O'Hara down the stairs and across the yard, and then, panting, said, "Stay here. Lie down. I'm going for help."

13

Kate took off as fast as she had ever run in her whole life. "Fire, fire!" she screamed, running. Her sides ached from running so fast, but she kept on running, shouting even louder, "Fire at the church!" Lights appeared in a few houses. People shouted out the windows, "What is it?" and she yelled back, "Fire at the church!" She ran up the stairs of her house and into Patrick's room. "Fire in the church!" she screamed.

Patrick jumped out of bed. "What?"

"Ma and I went there to bring the altar cloth and . . .

ah . . . some men came and started a fire and she's lying
outside at the edge of the yard and . . ."

He had his trousers on and was limping down the stairs.
She started after him. Clare was yelling, "What happened?" Kate stopped and shouted back, "There's a fire at
the church. Stay here with the children or come and help
—I don't know!" She ran after Patrick.

Others were running down the street now too. Everyone was shouting. Children were crying. Kate thought her
lungs would burst. Bells were ringing. She lost sight of
Patrick. There was a terrible panic in the air.

She ran faster.

"What happened?" Kate heard someone shout.

"The Know-Nothings set fire to the church!" she yelled.

"Can we save it?" someone else shouted. She didn't
answer.

Kate reached the path, turned, and saw great bursts of
orange flame flashing and flying out of the stained-glass
windows, which had been shattered. People were everywhere, screaming, shouting, and passing buckets of water.

"Where are the fire engines?" Kate yelled to a woman
running past her.

"Get in line and grab a bucket," the woman yelled
back.

Kate ran over to the end of a line. Someone passed her a
bucket of water, which she passed on. Over and over the
buckets came and Kate passed them down the line. Her
heart was beating madly, and she experienced a depth of
fear she had never known. She slipped out of the bucket

line and ran up to the church. She didn't know why, but she had a feeling that something even worse than the fire was going to happen. She pushed herself through the men nearest the front steps, just in time to see Patrick opening the front door. Flames were licking out around him.

"Patrick!" she screamed at the top of her voice.

He turned.

"Don't go in there!"

"Mother's inside!" he yelled, and then he slipped inside.

Nora rushed up, breathless. "Where's Patrick?" she yelled.

"He just went inside!" Kate screamed.

"Somebody fetch Patrick!" Nora wailed. "Somebody get him! He's inside the church and he'll be burned alive!" Nora's eyes were popping out and her face was white. "Somebody get him!" she wailed again and fainted to the ground. Kate looked around hysterically. No one was going up the steps to get Patrick.

She put her hands on her skirt and tore it down from her waist with one incredibly strong push. She ripped the material free from every seam that held it in place and, stepping over Nora, rushed it over to a bucket of water being passed to the church. She dipped the fabric in the water and put it over her head and shoulders like a shawl. She ran up the steps to the church.

"Somebody stop her!" a man yelled, but she was already inside. The heat sucked her breath away and for a moment she thought she had died. Then she saw a shape ahead in the smoke and flames.

"Patrick!"

He was staggering toward her, carrying a body.

"Patrick!" she yelled again, running toward him. Just at that moment she saw him fall to the ground. Mother O'Hara rolled on the floor. Kate couldn't look at her. She grabbed Patrick's arm, pulling him up and dragging him to the door.

"But Mother!" he cried, pulling back.

"She's dead," yelled Kate, "and if you don't get out of here, you'll be dead too!" Something hot fell on her shoulder and she screamed, pushing it away. With all her strength she shoved Patrick, sobbing, out the front door of the church and down the steps. Someone threw painfully icy water on her as she fell to the ground.

When Kate came to, she was lying on the sofa in the sitting room at the O'Haras'. She felt as if she were covered in hot stiff plastic, but it was only her skin. She moved slightly and felt the cold heat of the burns on her body. Her hands were covered with wet bandages. She opened her eyes.

"What happened?" she murmured, feeling her lips blistered.

"Ah, Kate, thank God, you're awake!" Clare leaned over and gave Kate a kiss on the forehead. "Would you like a sip of water?"

The water was cool and delicious, and slowly Kate realized that she was not seriously hurt. Her hands and a patch on her back were the worst. The rest was like a terrible, terrible sunburn. She shut her eyes and asked, half praying, "Is Patrick all right?"

"Aye, Kate," said Clare, "but Ma—" Clare burst into tears.

"I know," said Kate, shutting her eyes. "I know." A lump in her throat grew and seemed to burst as she remembered leaving Mother O'Hara on the floor. "She . . . she went back to get the lace. I didn't think . . . I told her to lie down outside."

"Say no more, Kate," said Clare. She put her hand on Kate's arm. "I know y' did the best you could."

Clare put her head down on the sofa and sobbed. With her bandaged hand Kate tried to pat her head as she sobbed too.

Patrick entered the room. He looked awful. "What happened to your hair?" Kate asked.

"The same thing that happened to yours," he said, kneeling down on the floor beside her. His hair was singed. The top of each strand was frizzy and red. His eyebrows and lashes were burned. His face was puffy and red.

Kate put her hand to her head, but because of the bandages she couldn't feel her hair.

"Is mine the same way?" she asked.

"Aye," said Patrick.

"Ah, Patrick," cried Kate, putting her arms out to him. Then, remembering herself, she stopped.

"It's all right, Kate," he said gently. "Clare, would you go out and mind Bridget and Michael? Take them for a walk. I'd like to talk with Kate."

Clare left the room.

Patrick looked at Kate sadly and said, "Y' came into the church after me." He swallowed and took a deep, shaky breath. He stood and walked stiffly across the room to get a stool. He set it on the floor next to Kate and sat down again, stretching his long legs out awkwardly.

Kate curled her legs up to make more room on the sofa. "Why don't you sit here?" she asked.

Patrick moved to the sofa, and Kate pulled her legs in closer so her feet wouldn't touch his leg. She didn't want to scare him again.

"The church burned down." He stopped, then continued. "We have nothing left, Kate, except the foundation." Patrick shut his eyes and made the same sound of trying to catch his breath again. Kate realized he was crying.

"Oh, Patrick," she whispered.

"Mother is dead," he went on. "I tried to save her, Kate. If only she hadn't gone in there, she would still be alive."

"I know," said Kate. She wanted to hug Patrick but she didn't dare. She saw him take a long drink from a tin cup she hadn't noticed he was holding before. She wished she could think of something to say that made sense, but it didn't seem to matter. There was a certain resolve about Patrick, as if he had rehearsed what he wanted to say.

He took another drink. "Kate," he said, "Mother was dead when you saw me carrying her. I just didn't want her to burn." This was too much for him. His shoulders shook and his face was contorted, but he didn't look away.

"Ah, Patrick" was all Kate was able to say.

"She died on the altar, Kate, I want y' to know that. The Lord in Heaven knows it's the one thought that cheers me. I found her collapsed there with the lace in her arms. Of all the wonderful places to pass away, the altar of God must be the very finest." He wiped his puffed red eyes and took another long drink. "To be sure, Kate, she is at rest beside the Virgin Mother in Heaven."

"Aye, Patrick," said Kate.

"Aye." Patrick hesitated, then went on. "There's one more thing, Kate. When I found her, she was still alive, and I must tell you what she said."

"What?" asked Kate, trying to sit up.

"First she blessed me and all of us by name. You last. And then she said, 'Patrick, there's something odd about Kate. She's not my daughter.'"

Kate dropped back on the pillow and felt her body flash with heat. Oh, Mother O'Hara, bless you. Thank God, he finally knows. She opened her eyes and saw Patrick take another long swallow.

She struggled to sit up. Her back hurt, but once she stopped moving, it felt better. She looked at Patrick and didn't know what to say. Now that he knew she wasn't his sister, she felt strangely shy.

"The wake for Mother is this afternoon," Patrick said, changing the subject. He also seemed embarrassed by the truth.

"Did others die?" she asked.

"No, thank God," he said. "But plenty were burned, and everyone is heartbroken with grief." He took a long drink, then seemed to get up the courage to say the last part of his speech.

"Kate," he said, putting out his hand on hers. His fingers were blistered, and several were bandaged together. "I'm sorry I ignored you those days before the fire." He stopped and swallowed. "Truth be told, that night in my room I wanted you, and I was sure it was the worst sin in the world, being we were brother and sister."

"Patrick!" Kate threw her arms around him, and he put his around her. They hugged so tight, it was as if the fire they felt in their burned skins welded them together.

"Hello! Anybody home?" It was Nora. By the time she entered the room, Kate and Patrick were sitting straight up at opposite ends of the sofa.

"Kate! You're awake! How are you?" Nora rushed over and put her arms around Kate's shoulders. "Can I fetch you anything? Do you want me to rub salve on your burns or fix you something to eat?" She turned to Patrick. "And how are you, my darling?" She kissed him on the cheek.

"I'll get you some broth. Just wait there. Don't try to come into the kitchen." When Nora left the room, Kate stared straight ahead. She couldn't look at Patrick and knew he couldn't look at her.

What will happen now? she wondered. Will we go back to work with these burns? Will the church get rebuilt? Will Patrick and I . . .

Kate, she said to herself with a strange sort of new-found wisdom, what will happen now is that Nora will bring us soup. She will spoon-feed it to us because she's the type who would like to do that. And we will drink it because we're hungry and need it. Then we will get up and go to Mother O'Hara's wake. That is what will happen now.

14

Kate was right about everything, except there was no need to go to the wake because the wake came to them. The house slowly filled with everyone Kate had ever met in the mill. They packed themselves into the parlor, the kitchen, and the yard. There must have been a hundred people come to mourn the death of Mother O'Hara. One by one they came to pay their respects to Patrick, Kate, and the other children. Bridget and Michael sat on the sofa between Kate and Patrick. Clare sat in a separate stuffed chair the whole time. She stared at each person with dark, tired eyes and never said a word.

Kate ached and felt suffocated. She wished she could go outside and feel the cool breeze on her face, but she knew she had to stay inside and greet people. She was a member of the family, after all.

"If we could only see Madeline's face again," Mick said when he passed by. "It's a shame she couldn't be laid out here for us to kiss."

Kate thought that was a creepy idea, but she did wish she could have seen Mother O'Hara one last time. In one night she had come to love this mother of the past, the only person who had sensed who she was—or wasn't. At least you won't have to cough anymore, Mother O'Hara. And you're with your husband at long last. Kate was surprised to find how easy it was to believe in Heaven.

Some women sat down on the floor in the corner of the room and started to cry out loud. Actually they weren't just crying, they were howling out in high-pitched voices like coyotes in the movies. Kate couldn't believe it. The women sounded crazy, but they didn't look crazy; in fact, one of them was Mother O'Hara's friend, Mrs. Mac-Mahon, the one who wrote everyone's letters back to Ireland.

This woman threw back her head and, raising her voice even higher, started to chant some words Kate couldn't understand. The other women chanted with her. They're like witches, Kate thought. And this is like a play. Clare stopped rocking and went over to the women. She curled up in her mother's friend's arms and let herself be held. The weird, high chanting took on a strangely comforting sound as Kate began to understand it was part of a ritual. Keening, she heard someone call it. The women shrieked louder and Kate glanced at Patrick, who was looking very proud. Maybe the more noise the women made, the more they loved the deceased person. If that was the case, Patrick had reason to be proud.

The wake went on and on, but most of the people had finished paying their respects to the family, so Kate no longer had to shake hands and tell people how she was feeling. She didn't have to listen to them say how brave she was, which she hadn't actually minded, but she was beginning to get tired of smiling and saying thank you, thank you, thank you. She rested back against the sofa and watched people mill around. She listened to the women and looked out the window. The yard was full of people eating and drinking. Kate shut her eyes and felt Bridget lean against her. Oh, Bridget, Kate thought, I love the way you take me for granted and come over to cuddle up any time you want. You make me feel so good.

Kate still didn't look much at Patrick. Had he really told her a while ago he knew she wasn't his sister? Had they really hugged? It seemed ages ago that that had happened. She felt as if she had been greeting people on the sofa for days. Gradually she became aware of sounds other than the wailing of the women. There was music outside and laughter. She looked out the window and saw people dancing. The wake had turned into a party.

Someone brought her a glass of whiskey. She looked around. All the people her age and older were drinking whiskey. The shrieking women were drinking whiskey. Nora came by, and even she was drinking whiskey. Kate took a sip. Agh! It was awful.

"Go ahead, Kate, it will make you feel better," Patrick said. Kate looked at him.

"Drink whiskey?" she asked.

"Mother wouldn't have minded, this time," he said, smiling the smile that was still wonderful even if his eyebrows were burned off. "Mick brought ten bottles. They were smuggled in from Hartford with the last stained-glass windows."

It took Kate about an hour of teeny sipping to get the whole glass down, but it didn't matter. There was no hurry. No one was going anywhere except in and out and over to see the women in the corner. People were laughing and crying and hugging each other frequently.

In a way Kate was horrified that people would get drunk at a funeral, yet on the other hand, they stayed respectful. They never stopped speaking of Mother O'Hara.

"She was a saint," said one woman to Kate.

"Bless her soul," said another. "She loved her family, her church, and Mother Ireland. She never stopped thinking about how she would take everyone back to County Kerry someday."

"And always feeling so poorly too," said the first.

Outside, people were singing sad and beautiful Irish songs. Kate thought she heard a bagpipe and decided to see. She rose painfully and stiffly.

"Take my arm?" Patrick said.

At first she thought to say no, but then she realized it made sense for him to help his sister. Arm in arm they went out to listen.

In the middle of a circle of men playing fiddles and mandolins was Uncle Mick pumping a small bagpipe. It seemed to Kate as if she were hearing two tunes at the same time. The high tune was happy and it made Kate glad she was standing beside Patrick, holding on to his arm. The other sound, though, was low and droning. It lay beneath the fast melody like the sadness in Kate's heart. Mother O'Hara was dead.

The tune ended.

"Sure he's the finest uilleann piper in America," said Patrick quietly.

Uncle Mick held his elbows still and looked around, waiting until everyone was quiet, even the children. Eventually the only sound that could be heard was the keening of the women inside.

"Last night," he said softly, "our church was burned and my sister Madeline O'Hara died." His quiet words and huge presence commanded everyone's attention. "Madeline O'Hara," he continued, raising his voice, "was born in 1810, in Cahersiveen, County Kerry, Ireland. She came to America in 1846 to escape the potato famine. She came with her husband and five children, including Bridget, a two-year-old babe at the time. Her husband, Patrick Michael O'Hara, died aboard ship from ship fever, God rest his soul. Madeline worked all her life. Last night she died."

With his hands clasped around his bagpipe, Uncle Mick

shut his eyes and bowed his head. The others were silent and bowed their heads too.

Kate shut her eyes to hold back tears. She heard everyone move. They were kneeling. Father Tully had come forward to pray.

"God Almighty," the priest shouted. "We now have no roof under which to assemble other than the broad canopy of Heaven. Will You still hear our prayer? We know You will. Father, we commend to You Madeline O'Hara, our friend and relative, a saint among us, may she rest in peace. God's blessing be with her soul, and give her the everlasting repose of Heaven and our own souls at the last day." His voice stayed high and intense. "Heavenly Father, help us lift our heads and our hearts from this tragedy and find our way in this country, O Lord. Most of all, blessed Jesus, give us the strength to rebuild our church! Amen!"

"Let's start today!" someone shouted over the echo of amens.

"Yes, today!" Patrick shouted. Kate looked at him. His face was full of excitement.

"We'll double the guard," James shouted.

"And this time we'll build out of stone," said Uncle Mick.

The idea caught on so quickly that within minutes everyone had decided to go to the church to start work. Kate and Patrick started to follow.

"Where do you think you two are going?" asked Uncle Mick. He was coming out of the house with the keeners.

"Y' must stay here and rest. Begorra, ye've done enough."

"I'll stay here with them," said Nora, running over.

"To tell ye the truth, Nora," said Uncle Mick, "I'd like you to come with me to the church. There's something I want to ask you. When you were in the weaving room with Madeline, did you ever hear her speak of . . ." Kate watched Nora leave reluctantly with Mick.

She looked at Patrick and Patrick looked at her.

They went in and started to clean up, but there was nothing they could do in their condition.

"What I'd like to do, God's truth, is lie down," said Patrick.

"Aye," said Kate. I don't believe this is happening, she said to herself.

They went upstairs to Patrick's room and lay like two decrepit old folks on his narrow bed. Kate rested her bandaged hands on her stomach and couldn't help laughing. It must be the whiskey, she thought, somewhat embarrassed. Patrick laughed too.

"Who are you, then?" he asked with a shy smile.

She had never told him her last name.

"Kate Calambra," she said, giggling. She felt awful to be feeling silly, but she couldn't help it.

"Kate who?"

"Kate Calambra. My father is Italian, but I'm Irish on my mother's side. I live in this town the way it is in the nineteen eighties, Patrick."

"Aye?" His voice was soft, questioning, ready, she thought.

"Yes! Oh, you wouldn't believe it! All the streets are paved and the people ride in cars and . . . and, oh, if only I could bring you back there with me! You wouldn't have to work in a cotton mill. You could go to school and play on the baseball team and . . ." A wave of homesickness passed over her.

"Stop." Patrick rested a bandaged hand on one of Kate's. "Kate," he said. "Please, for the love of God, don't tell me such strange things now. Ye are not my sister, that I know, but I'm too confused to hear of other devilments now."

"But—"

"Give me a little time."

Neither of them spoke. Kate felt tired, sore, and a little impatient. She wanted to tell Patrick everything, but he wouldn't let her. She lay still and must have slept, for when she heard the voices of the mourners returning from church, the sun was low in the sky.

15

At the church site the mourners had received a surprise visit. Mr. Harris had driven up in a chaise drawn by two white horses and delivered a short, brisk speech from his seat. He and Mr. Lancaster wanted to express their sorrow for the tragedy. Mr. Lancaster would donate half of the cost of rebuilding the church. Unless operatives were severely injured, they were to report for work the next day.

Everyone was pleased about the offer of financial help for the church.

"Ah, they just want to show the Yankees we're here to stay," said Patrick sarcastically.

Kate was surprised to hear him say a few minutes later that he'd be going to work Monday. She drew him aside.

"What about your burns, Patrick?"

"Ah, they won't hurt any more than my leg did last week," he said. "We need the money. We won't be having your wage this week and we won't have Ma's anymore at all."

"But doesn't she have insurance and don't you get sick pay?" she asked.

"What's that?"

"Money that comes to the family after someone dies."

"That's sick pay?"

"No, that's insurance! Sick pay is when you get paid even if you're home sick."

Patrick looked at her strangely. "Don't be joking with me, Kate."

Kate realized that to Patrick the idea that a boss would pay a man for work he didn't do was ludicrous. To tell him such things somehow made him feel defensive.

"What will I do with myself all week?" she asked, changing the subject and thinking wistfully about TV for the first time since she'd left home.

"I don't know," said Patrick. "Too bad y' can't read."

"Patrick! Of course I can read!"

Again he thought she was joking, but this time the truth was easy to prove.

"Give me something to read and I'll show you."

Patrick looked around the room. "We don't have anything because none of us can read. Ma used to take her letters to—wait, I'll get the ones she received from Ireland!"

In a glass jar in the pantry was a roll of well-thumbed letters resting on a small pile of coins.

"Here, Kate," said Patrick doubtfully. "Can you read these?"

Kate picked up a letter. It was poorly written and the grammar was terrible, but she tried to read it smoothly.

" 'Dear Madeline,' " she began. " 'How's yourself? And how's the children? God bless, it's four years now since I last seen you walking down the road. Thank you for sending more money for my passage.' "

Patrick was incredulous. "Kate, how do you do that?"

Kate swallowed. She didn't want to embarrass him more, but she had to get across to him the true fact that she really did come from another time. "Patrick, where I come from, practically everyone can read, even little children Bridget's age."

"God's truth, Kate," said Patrick nervously, "if you suddenly show everyone here you can read, they'll think you're bewitched. Now, for this week I'll get you some newspapers and books from Mrs. MacMahon, but say that you're looking at the pictures in them, aye?"

"Aye," said Kate, smiling.

Patrick looked down at the floor. She had embarrassed him again.

"Would ye teach me to read?" he finally asked in a low voice.

"Of course," said Kate. "Every evening after the others have gone to bed. You'll learn in no time."

All day Monday she rested and read. Mrs. MacMahon's books were too wordy and overdetailed for Kate's taste, but she loved reading the newspapers. They were a week old, she reckoned, but it didn't matter. They told her about the year 1850.

She read about the gold rush in California and how people all over the East were still leaving to seek their fortunes. She read about a huge mill city in Massachusetts named Lowell that employed thousands of workers from all over New England, mostly girls about her age. That's where Nora should go, she thought with a smile. The President of the United States was Zachary Taylor. Kate couldn't remember a thing about him from her history courses.

Kate was fascinated by accounts of runaway slaves being caught and returned to their masters. There was a lot of outrage expressed in the paper toward something called the Fugitive Slave Act, which had just been passed. The law made it hard for Northerners to help the slaves. If a slave came to your back door in the middle of the night and you gave him a cup of coffee, you could be fined and thrown in jail.

Kate searched the paper for mention of Abraham Lincoln and found none. The only famous name she recognized was Ulysses S. Grant, who at the time was a subordinate to President Taylor. His name made her feel both sad and excited, sad because she knew the Civil War was coming, and excited because she was the only one alive who knew about it. She was dying to show Grant's name to Patrick and tell him what she knew.

That evening, however, she hardly got a chance to speak to him. Nora had come home with the family for supper and, without being asked, had taken over Mother O'Hara's role.

"Bridget, wash up, then lie down and rest until your supper's ready. Michael, fetch some wood. Clare, set out the plates. Kate, how was your day?" Without waiting for Kate's answer, she turned to Patrick. "Patrick, would y' like me to change the bandage on your leg? Or rub salve on your hands?"

"I—I can do it myself, Nora," said Patrick. He went up to his room with a red face.

It made Kate mad the way Nora was carrying on, but what could she do about it? With her hands bandaged up she couldn't set the table, cook, or do dishes. Exasperated, she went into the parlor and sat down.

"Are you all right?" Clare had come in.

"I'm fine, Clare," said Kate. "How was work?"

" 'Twas a bit hard today, Kate."

Kate felt so sorry that Clare and everyone else had to go back to the mill after supper that she forgot to stay mad at Nora, but when Nora came back with the family after work was over for the day, Kate felt annoyed again.

"God love you, Kate. Why don't ye go to bed? I'll help the children," said Nora a little too cheerfully.

Kate sighed and trudged upstairs. She waited in bed

until Patrick walked Nora home. Then she went downstairs and waited for him.

"Patrick, are ye ready for your lesson?" He looked tired but she showed him Grant's name anyway. "G-R-A-N-T. That spells Grant, Patrick. Learn that word, because he's going to be important. There's going to be war over slavery. I'm not sure when it starts but I think it's around 1860. The North will beat the South and a man named Abraham Lincoln will free the slaves!"

Patrick looked at her uncomfortably, but he repeated after her, "Grant. G-R-A-N-T."

"And look here. L-O-W-E-L-L. That spells Lowell. It's a huge place with many more mills than we have here. Girls from all over New England run away to work there." She didn't mention her thought about Nora working there.

"Aye, I've heard of Lowell. When we first came to America, we almost went there, but then we heard how big it was and we were afraid.

"We were so ignorant, Kate. We didn't know one mill from another, less how to work in them. All I knew was how to cut peat and plant potatoes, the way my father had taught me. There was none of that work here. And Da so recently dead, we didn't know what to do. I can tell you as a fact we were hard put to keep ourselves alive."

Kate didn't know why Patrick had chosen this moment during his reading lesson to tell her about his father, but she sat back and listened carefully, for Patrick was speaking with a tight, low voice.

"My da was a big man, Kate, and he was the best dancer in County Kerry. When Uncle Mick played, he danced all night. He was so strong, no one could have believed that aboard ship, during the duration of that thirty-day journey, he would become so weak. He couldn't eat, Kate, couldn't move."

Patrick cracked his knuckles and looked away.

Kate was quiet. Maybe he wanted to tell her about his world as much as she wanted to tell him about hers.

"He died the day before we landed. Mother was so grieved, she wouldn't stop keening. Americans thought she had brain fever so she had to stop." Patrick looked suddenly at Kate. "They'll think you've got it too, Kate, if y' tell them you're from the nineteen eighties. Pray God, Kate, don't tell anyone else what you're telling me!"

Kate looked at Patrick and saw how serious he was.

"Patrick," she said. "Ye are the only one who knows about me. I'll not be telling anyone else. Y' tell me about your world and I'll tell you about mine. Nobody else will know what we say."

"Tomorrow night," said Patrick, "after I take Nora home, we'll talk again." He rose and gave her a smile: not a full one—he was feeling too sad for that. But it was enough for Kate to know he had true feelings for her.

"Where do ye live?" he asked her quietly the next night. They were sitting on the porch where she had waited for him.

Kate was eager to tell him. "I live on the other side of

town, in South Lancaster. I don't know if that's been built yet."

"Sure, that's where most of the Yankees live and where the silk mill is, about eight miles from here. I've been there once or twice. They're not hiring Irish yet, but they will. I hear they're building a new mill."

"I live in a yellow house and I don't have any brothers or sisters. I have a room of my own. It has two big windows and white curtains—"

"Are ye rich?"

"Well, not exactly. But compared to you, I guess you would say we are."

"What do you mean?"

"Well, take my father. He works in an insurance company, but he only works from ten to six. The rest of the time he plays tennis and goes fishing and fixes things around the house. He has more free time to have fun than people here."

"Tennis?"

"That's when two people stand on opposite sides of a net and hit a ball back and forth to each other with a racket."

"Sounds like something rich folks would do. What about your ma?"

"She restores old houses and sells antiques."

"Antiques?"

"Old furniture. Take your bed. It's a cast iron bed. What do you think's going to happen to it? The mattress will wear out but the iron won't. Someday my mother could find your bed in someone's attic and sell it for a hundred dollars."

"Kate, stop joking with me!"

"I'm not! Honest! I'm not kidding." Without realizing it, Kate had dropped her Irish accent completely.

"What's 'kidding'?"

"Joking."

" 'Kidding.' I thought kidding was having baby goats." Patrick started to laugh. "God bless you, Kate, I like to hear the way you really talk. Say some more."

Kate laughed too. "Okay. I'm a sophomore in high school. I can't stand gym, but I was thinking of going out for cheerleading this fall if the gym teacher isn't in charge. She's a real nerd."

Patrick's eyes sparkled. "And now I'm going to say something to you in Gaelic."

"What's Gaelic?"

"That's the language of Ireland. What we speak today is English with an Irish accent because the bloody English took over our country and oppressed it for hundreds of years. But before they came, Kate, we had a beautiful language. Listen."

Patrick looked Kate in the eyes and said very softly, "*Mavourneen dheelish.*"

The words gave Kate a thrill. "What does that mean?" she asked quietly.

"My sweet darling," he said. "Ma used to say it to us when we were little. Just now I—I wanted to say it to you."

Patrick seemed so self-conscious, he didn't move. Kate longed to move closer to him, but she sensed that if she did, she would push Patrick away. He seemed to be fighting some kind of mental battle inside.

After a long silence he sighed. "I wonder what my real sister is doing now."

"I think she must live in my house," Kate said.

Patrick seemed surprised and also relieved to have something not so personal to talk about. "You mean she's somewhere in the future? She doesn't have to work?"

"I think so," said Kate. "Right at this moment she could be sleeping in my bed or out with . . . some of my friends." Kate was going to say Warren, but she didn't want to tell Patrick about him. "I hope she doesn't stack my records," Kate said out of the blue.

"What does that mean?"

"Oh, they're . . ." But Kate couldn't think of how to explain them. Flat discs like a plate and you put it on a machine that goes round and round and out comes music? She was too tired. "They're like musical instruments," she said.

By Thursday night Patrick had prepared a whole series of questions for Kate. He wanted to hear about the war all over again, so she told him again, remembering this time about the Emancipation Proclamation. She even recited a few lines of it.

Patrick seemed most interested when she told him facts about factory workers and Catholics. She told him not to worry about the fate of the Irish in America. She told him

that in 1960 an Irish Catholic named John Fitzgerald
Kennedy would be elected President of the United States.

"And nobody stones him? Nobody burns his house? I
can't believe a Catholic could get to be President in this
country without a sore lot of trouble."

"Well, there is trouble. He gets assassinated. So does
President Lincoln."

"I told you!" Patrick said. "I could have guessed that.
Lincoln gets killed because he frees the slaves and Kennedy because he's Catholic. I tell you in this country they
don't like anybody different."

"No, Patrick, that's not so. Kennedy doesn't get shot
because he's a Catholic, and neither does his brother.
They get shot because—"

"His brother gets shot too?"

"Yes, but—"

"Kate, you may know *what* happens in the future, but
you don't seem to understand why. You can't tell me that
in America an Irish Catholic gets elected President and
then both he and his brother get shot and killed for another reason. Why else would they get shot?"

For the life of her, Kate couldn't come up with an answer. She vaguely remembered something about a con-
spiracy and wished she knew more about it.

On Friday she took her bandages off. Her shoulder and
hands were rough and raw but better. She helped Nora
with the cooking and even said at one point as politely as
she could, "You won't be needing to come here every
evening now, Nora."

"Aye," said Clare. "Kate and I can be doing Ma's job ourselves now."

Kate looked at her and had a sudden flash that Clare didn't like Nora anymore. She wondered why. Perhaps it was because after Mother O'Hara's death her children had pulled together instinctively, and now they resented an outsider among them. Perhaps Clare sensed that Patrick no longer cared for Nora.

That night it was pouring outside, and Kate and Patrick sat up talking in the parlor. Kate was telling him about the astronauts and he was laughing.

"Y' say they put a flag on the moon?"

"Yes," said Kate.

"And left their rubbish there? Sure, Kate, I think it's lucky you're here where you can help us build the stone church. This world you come from sounds very queer."

She looked at Patrick's blue eyes flashing, and suddenly the skin on her back felt unbearably itchy. At first she tried to keep her mind off it, but then she could no longer stand it.

"What's the matter, Kate?"

"My back is so itchy, I can't stand it," she said. "The skin is peeling and my clothes rub against it."

"Can I do anything to help you?"

"Do you think you could rub some salve on it?" It was a bold suggestion, she could tell from the look on Patrick's face, but really it was no big deal to have a boy rub your back. When she went to the beach with Warren, he rubbed suntan lotion on her back.

"Rub it on your skin?"

"Aye, just sit there and I'll turn this way and loosen my dress." He didn't have to look, for God's sake.

It would have been better, of course, if her dress unfastened from the back, but it didn't. Kate untied the front laces and let it slip down to her waist. Her back and chest were only covered now by the thin linen slip, and the itching was worse because the dress had rubbed coming off. Kate shivered.

Holding her hands over her breasts the way she did in the doctor's office, she felt her nipples hard as upholstery tacks. Patrick was silent. He didn't touch her.

"Just rub it on, Patrick. I can't stand it!"

She heard him unscrew the lid of the jar and set the cap down. Then she felt the cool, relieving touch of the salve on her skin. Her shoulders stretched and her body shivered.

"Ah, Patrick, that feels wonderful!"

Gently he smoothed the salve over her burned shoulder. Kate lifted her shoulder blades. She loved the way his hand moved.

"Put some a little farther down," she said. "Reach under." She arched her back so there would be space for his hand under the slip. But he couldn't reach under, so Kate slipped the shift off her shoulders and let it drop to her waist. Patrick took a deep breath, then he started using both hands. He brought them up the center of her back and then over the shoulders and, holding his hands sideways, brought them down her back. His fingertips reached around and touched the edges of her breasts. He stopped.

"Kate," he whispered. "I—I think I love ye."

"Patrick," she cried softly, turning her body to his. She pressed against him and threw her arms around his neck. She thought she would die from the sweetness of his full embrace. Patrick brought his hands around to her front and touched her breasts again. Kate kissed his face and burrowed her face in his neck.

"Patrick," she murmured, "I think I love you too." An overpowering magnetism held her body tightly to his and made her squirm to get more comfortable. She unbuttoned his shirt so her flesh could touch his as his hands moved over her, gently, lovingly. No, not that, said a voice in Kate, that is too much, sit up now, cover yourself. But she couldn't stop. They were lying down now. Reaching, kissing, touching him in places she had never touched, she knew she wanted an even closer way to be.

He stopped first.

"Lord have mercy, Kate," he said, panting, pulling his hands away from her skirt, which he had started to lift up. "This is not proper." He wiped his wet hair off his brow.

Kate lay still with her head on his chest, shocked, her heart pounding like a caged beast. She didn't know what to say. She had never felt anything like this before. She didn't think she was old enough.

"Ah, Kate, I tell ye," Patrick whispered. "I mustn't. Not again. It's a sin, Kate. We mustn't, but, ah, Kate." Patrick drew her face up to his and kissed it softly.

She sat up, breathing hard, and, turning away from him,

put her arms back into her shift. He helped her with her dress, and when she was done, he took her hand and led her upstairs to her bedroom. He stopped at her door.

"Whoever you are, Kate, wherever you came from, I love you," he whispered. "We will figure something out."

16

"We will figure something out." She thought about his words all day Saturday. She couldn't read her newspapers, she was so busy carrying on a conversation inside between her worrying, questioning self and her brave, I'll-do-any-thing self.

If we get married, we could do what we started last night over and over again and it wouldn't be wrong.

But I'm only fifteen.

True, but this is in the past. Girls get married young here.

But people think we're brother and sister.

We could move somewhere where people don't know us.

But what about Clare, Bridget, and Michael?

They'll come with us. I'll tell them who I am.

They'll think I'm crazy!

Not if I show them I can read and that I know things. They won't think I'm crazy. They love me. Patrick will tell them what his mother said. I'll teach them to read so they can get good jobs when they grow up.

For the first time Kate was beginning to feel completely happy about staying in the past for good. It pained her to think she might not ever see her mother and father again, but at least they had the other Kate.

Kate felt more alive than she had ever felt. Though life was harder, she had to admit it was more exciting. She'd worked in a mill. She'd rescued someone in a fire. She'd held a real gun. Before, what had she ever done? Played records, watched TV, danced close with Warren at stupid parties.

Where will Patrick and I live?

The solution came to Kate late in the afternoon, and she could hardly wait until nighttime. If Patrick still felt the same way about her, she would tell him.

"We could go out west."

"What?" Patrick looked amazed. It was raining again, and they were sitting at the kitchen table because, without talking about it, they knew they couldn't trust themselves again alone in the parlor. Everyone else was asleep, and Nora had finally left after lingering for a long time.

As soon as he was back, Patrick had kissed Kate and told her she'd been on his mind all day at work. "I've never before had this feeling inside of me, Kate. Nora is wondering what to make of my mood and I don't know what to tell her. God Almighty, I don't know what to do!"

That's when Kate blurted out, "We could go out west." He was shocked.

"Don't you see, Patrick? We can't stay here hiding from everyone. I've been thinking about it all day. I know about the West. I've seen hundreds of shows about it and read books too. You could get a job on the railroads and I could teach school!"

Patrick's eyes lit up. "Y' mean we could be married some place where no one thinks we're brother and sister?"

Kate couldn't bring herself to say the word *married*, but yes, that's exactly what she was thinking. They could have an incredible adventure. Driving a Conestoga wagon, camping out on the prairies. She wasn't even afraid of the Indians. All they asked for was respect for their way of life. Why, she'd know just how to do it. They could fish. Maybe once the Indians were their friends, they would show them where the best fish were. They could hunt too. Maybe she'd even learn to shoot a gun.

"It wouldn't be easy, Kate. I've heard tell the railroad towns are lawless places. But if we could save enough money, we might make it all the way across the land to California. I could go looking for gold. I'd like to find so much, I could come back and build a mansion as big as

Mr. Lancaster's. Mother and Father could look down at us from Heaven . . . hm-m-m. I wonder if Ma will tell Da about us and if he'll understand. He never met you, y' know." Patrick looked amused. "But maybe they can see my sister Kate too. Maybe from up in Heaven they can see all of us.

"Kate," he said, suddenly changing the subject, "what about Bridget and Michael and Clare? Who will take care of them while we're gone?"

"They could stay with Uncle Mick. When we're settled, we'll send for them and then I'll tell them about myself."

"They'll never believe you."

"Why not? You do. I'll show them how I can read and I'll tell them things that will happen in the future. I'll show them how I can talk without an Irish accent. They'll believe me, Patrick, I know they will, because they love me!"

Patrick sighed, half-bewildered, half-excited. "And Nora?"

"You're going to have to tell her, Patrick, that you don't love her anymore."

"Aye, that's the truth of it."

"Tell her you've been so saddened, you can't think of her anymore. Tell her we're going out west to find a better life. Tell her you can't bear mill work anymore. Tell her you can't stand the new agent. Tell her to go to Lowell."

Patrick shook his head. He looked confused, yet his eyes were twinkling. "I tell ye, Kate, you're the most amazing thing that's ever happened to me. More amazing than coming to America." He grinned. "I surely would like to leave the mills and go to California." But then he frowned. "But to leave without proper revenge. Are ye sure ye didn't see who set the fire?"

Kate had been lying about this for a week now. "They had sacks over their heads."

"And ye can't remember any more details about them?"

"No. I was too scared. I can't even remember if they were tall or short. All I remember are the sacks, the guns, the straws, and the flint."

Patrick sighed and cracked his knuckles again. He looked at Kate, then away from her.

"We'll be all right," she said, putting her hand over his.

"But what if ye suddenly leave, Kate? And I find I'm in California with my sister?"

Kate swallowed. "It's a chance you'll have to take, Patrick. Would that be so bad?"

"Nae. At least we'd be out of the mills."

He was silent.

"But I'd sorely miss you, Kate," he said, looking away.

"I know," said Kate. "I'd miss you too. But don't think about it. I know I'm here for good."

The next day was Sunday, a day of rest for the workers. There was no Mass. Father Tully was an itinerant priest. He would not be coming to Lancaster for two more weeks.

Nora came over before breakfast. "I thought we could

work on the church together," she said to Patrick. She seemed edgy, as if she weren't well, yet trying to be cheerful anyway.

At the church Nora shadowed Patrick everywhere and made Kate furious. She couldn't stand to watch so she went off and found work to do with Clare. They carried stones from stone walls over to piles near the foundation. It was rough, exhausting work. Clare finally gave it up and joined others collecting smaller stones for another pile.

After a while Patrick came over to Kate, embarrassed. "I don't know what's the matter with Nora," he said.

"Aye?"

"She's acting so strange, almost as if she senses there's a feeling between us."

"How could she know?"

"She couldn't."

"Then don't worry about it." Kate's voice was sharper than she'd intended.

"Well, I've made up me mind. I can't stand how she hangs around me. I'm going to tell her tonight I don't care for her anymore."

"Good," said Kate, a little relieved. It wasn't that she doubted Patrick. Still.

"Kate."

"Aye?"

"Come now, look up at me."

She was trying to pick up a large flat stone. She stopped,

wiped her brow, and looked up. Patrick was smiling the smile that always opened her heart.

"Ah, Pat," she said, calling him the nickname his mother used to call him, "good luck with her tonight. I'll go to bed early so you'll be able to talk to her in private."

But as tired as she was, the thought of the two of them out there on the porch made sleep impossible. She lay in bed with her eyes wide open. Her fingers ached from working on the church. She heard Bridget fall asleep, then Clare. She tried not to listen to the voices that rose up from the porch.

There was a long silence, then the voices again. Another long silence. Voices again. Patrick and Nora were talking for a long time.

Kate couldn't help it. Despite her pledge to leave them alone, she climbed out of bed and tiptoed downstairs. She thought of the first time she had gone down those narrow stairs. Patrick had just finished putting on her shoes. How long ago was that? Only two weeks? Impossible. She felt as if she had known Patrick for years—a hundred and thirty-one years, to be exact. Perhaps it was the attraction they felt for each other that had pulled her out of time and space toward him. Two weeks, a hundred and thirty-one years, fifteen years old, eighteen years old. The numbers, under the circumstances, were meaningless.

She reached the bottom stair and stood there quietly in her bare feet. She heard nothing now. Not even a whisper. Maybe he just told Nora he doesn't love her anymore and she's shocked. She'll probably leave soon.

She heard Nora crying. Yes, he must have told her! Kate couldn't help herself. She felt joyous. She tiptoed closer to the door.

"I'm sorry, Patrick," she heard Nora say, half sobbing.

Patrick didn't say anything back. What was Nora sorry for?

"It wasn't the way I wanted it, I didn't know it would happen," Nora said.

"But I don't understand. I don't see how . . ." Patrick said, sounding very upset. Nora began to cry louder.

"Hush," said Patrick. "Hush, it's all right, Nora. It's going to be all right." His voice caught in his throat.

Kate's heart began to pound. What was going on? Why were they making such a big deal out of it? So he doesn't love her anymore! Come on, Patrick. Just get it over with. Make her go home. Don't let her cry on your shoulder.

There was a long silence during which Kate grew afraid. Something was wrong. Even without seeing him she knew Patrick had his jaw clamped tight. She heard him crack his knuckles all at once.

Kate bent over from the waist and touched her toes three times to shed some of the terrible energy that was building inside of her. Patrick! she felt like screaming. Get her out of here! What are you taking so long for! We're going to get married, remember! We're going out west!

At that moment Kate wanted to get married to Patrick more than anything she had ever wanted in her whole life. Far more than going back to the future. Far more than ever seeing her parents again.

"I've thought on it, Nora. By the grace of God, there's only one thing to do," she heard Patrick say. "We'll be wed when Father Tully comes again."

"Will ye tell him?"

"Aye, I'll not have us lying to a priest. We have committed a sin, and without the priest's blessing, the baby will be born under the Devil's curse."

Baby? What baby? What was Patrick talking about? But Kate knew the answer and she knew it absolutely. Fury shot through her body like lightning. She doubled over slowly, rigidly, as if half-paralyzed, bringing her fists down tightly through the air. She crouched on the floor like a stone statue. Machinelike, her fists moved up and down, pounding the air with all the strength she had, as if she could crush the truth into nothingness.

"No! No! No!" she silently screamed.

"Oh, Patrick," sobbed Nora. "I love you so much."

"Hush, Nora, hush, don't cry," Patrick said.

Kate rose fast now and raised her fists to the ceiling. Her eyes burned. Her throat hurt, and her heart was bursting. She knew she could not stay there another moment. She turned and ran up the stairs. She pulled on a dress and wrapped her apron in a shawl. After she heard Patrick walk down the street with Nora, she ran downstairs, took the money she'd seen in the letter jar, and stuffed it into her shawl. Then, racing through the night to the train depot, she collapsed in shock on the bench and waited. She would run away to Lowell.

Her rage was so monstrous that she couldn't have said

whether she waited five minutes or five hours for the train to Boston, but eventually, out of the dark of the night, it pulled into the station enveloped by a great whoosh of steam. A conductor stepped off, dropped a mail pouch on the ground, and was about to get back up on the train when he noticed her.

"What are you doing here?"

"I'm going to Lowell," said Kate and then, seeing his face, added, "I've money for me fare."

"Lowell, eh? Hop on. You'll be there in about four and a half hours. Change trains at Boston."

Kate climbed aboard. The train was only half-full and everyone on it was asleep. She picked a seat on the side of the train that didn't face the O'Haras' part of town. Sitting rigid, she held her breath as the train pulled out of Lancaster.

The conductor came by.

"That'll be a one-way ticket?"

"Aye?"

"One-way?"

For a moment, she couldn't answer. To say yes was to acknowledge she was leaving everyone she knew and was going somewhere she'd never been. She looked at the conductor and nodded.

"Fifty cents," he said. "If you don't have it, miss, you'll have to get off at the next station."

Numbly Kate reached into her shawl and took out the money. "I have it," she said, handing it to the conductor.

The conductor gave her a ticket and walked down the aisle.

Now that it was final, Kate burst into tears. "Patrick, I despise you!" she whispered, trying to keep her shaky sobs quiet.

She lay down on the seat, put her hands and her shawl under her head, and cried herself to sleep.

17

Someone shook her shoulder.

"Come, miss, sit up," he said. It was the conductor. "We're almost to Boston."

"What?" Kate was bewildered. Oh, God. She remembered everything.

"Can you tell me how to get the Lowell train?" she asked shakily.

"Get the Boston-Lowell express on Track Three. It leaves at three fifty A.M. You'll have time to get a good seat if you go right along."

"Thank you," said Kate, tying her bonnet beneath her chin. She tried to smile.

"Know anyone there, do you?" the conductor asked.

"No, I'm afraid not," she said meekly.

The conductor scrunched his eyebrows down and looked at her sympathetically. "It's not easy to get a job if you don't know anyone," he said.

She didn't say anything.

"I tell you what. You look like a decent young lady. Go to Boardinghouse Number Two. My second cousin, Widow Smith, is the housemistress there. Tell her you met me on the train. I've sent her girls like you before. She won't be surprised."

"Thank you," said Kate. For the first time the conductor smiled.

"Come along," he said. "I'll help you carry your trunk."

"I . . . I don't have one," said Kate, embarrassed.

"You don't have a trunk? Where are your things?"

She looked down at her shawl.

The conductor shook his head and said, "Well, I hope Widow Smith helps you out. She don't look kindly on girls with suspicious backgrounds."

"Oh, I'm not suspicious, sir," said Kate, and then to convince him she added, "I can read."

"Good luck, miss," he called.

Kate looked down the platform toward the other part of the station. It was fairly dark. The only lights were oil lanterns that hung on alternate iron columns reaching up to a dark high ceiling. The few people she saw were men. There were no other girls her age.

"Oh, Patrick, how could you?" Kate whispered into the cavernous space. She stepped forward miserably and walked toward the front of the train. The train station was huge, and when she reached the main waiting room, she realized she had been there before. This was the same station her family arrived in when they went to Red Sox games! The huge columns and vaulted doorways were exactly the same, except cleaner and roomier somehow. There were no magazine stands and hot dog vendors crowding them.

A sign said "Tracks 1–5 this way" and had an arrow pointing to the left. Kate walked in that direction, wishing for the first time in days that she could see her mother and father again. But it was a hopeless wish, so hopeless, she thought she might just give up altogether and collapse on the marble floor. She made her feet move, one after the other, until she found Track 3 and saw a big black train smoking on its tracks, ready to leave.

"Is this the train to Lowell?" she asked the conductor, knowing it was but trying to postpone the moment she would actually have to board it. She felt faint.

"Sure is, miss. Say, are you all right?"

Kate opened her eyes.

"All aboard!" the conductor hollered over her head.

Kate found a seat by a window and fell into it. She huddled against the wall and wrapped her shawl about her tightly. Maybe I never really loved him, she thought. Maybe it was just a silly, stupid crush. I never really even got to know what he was like. To think that he and Nora had . . . and I didn't even know. Oh!

She felt humiliated and unclean. She couldn't stand to think he had touched her. *Mavourneen dheelish*, my eye, Kate thought angrily. He probably said that to her too. When I told him I loved him, he was probably laughing inside. He probably started thinking how he could take advantage of me the first time I told him I was from the future. He probably thought I was a mental basket case. He probably has no morals at all.

She stared out the window, cursing Patrick silently and watching a cloudy dawn pale the countryside. As the morning light increased, though, her rage seemed to diminish. Every time the train passed through a small mill town like Lancaster, she found the workers' houses and thought she saw Patrick's face looking for her from a window.

It was no use. No matter how she tried, she couldn't work up a lasting, convincing case against him. For the truth was, he had never tried to take advantage of her, and she knew it.

She rested her head against the cold, bumpy window and thought about the quiet times they had had together when their burns were healing and the night they almost . . . oh! He must have not wanted to do that with her, especially knowing that he had done it with Nora and that it had been a sin.

Kate played back Patrick's voice when he said to Nora, "I've thought on it, Nora. By the grace of God, there's only one thing to do. We'll be wed when Father Tully comes again." This time Kate heard distinctly how his voice had cracked on the word "married." "We have committed a sin and without the priest's blessing, the baby will be born under the Devil's curse."

With a twist in her heart Kate heard how Patrick had hesitated before the word "baby" and how he had sighed afterward. If he was anything, Patrick was moral. He had made a mistake and now he was willing to pay for it.

But then an awful thought occurred to Kate. What if Nora wasn't really pregnant? Kate grabbed the armrest and held on with both hands. She shut her eyes and bit her cheeks. She wouldn't let Nora get away with it. As soon as she arrived in Lowell, she would go back and convince Patrick to wait until the fall to see if Nora got fat.

But Kate knew Patrick wouldn't do that. It didn't matter whether Nora was pregnant or not. If she told Patrick she was, she would shame him into marrying her.

Besides, Kate had no money for a return-trip ticket. Her heart felt pressed into a small cold metal box. There was nothing, absolutely nothing she could do.

The train was slowing down. Kate looked out the window and saw a huge mill town ahead. A better word for it would have been mill city. Everywhere were mills and canals. There wasn't just one bell tower. There were dozens of them. There were fifty times as many buildings as there were in Lancaster. They were all made of brick and in the gray-green sunrise they looked like part of an evil red city deposited in the middle of the countryside by a wicked witch.

The Lowell train station was smaller than the one in

Boston. People were awake and about. Kate saw other girls her age getting off other trains. They seemed to know where to go. Sadly she followed them out onto the sidewalk and saw them turn left, down a street next to a long canal.

Three-story buildings lined the street on the opposite side. They had little colonial windows and short slanting roofs. "Boardinghouse No. 1" said a black and gold sign on the first one. Kate stopped and stared at the second building, "Boardinghouse No. 2." This must be the one the conductor had told her to go to. She heard girls singing from one of the windows upstairs and stepped closer to hear.

> *"I do not like my overseer,*
> *I do not mean to stay,*
> *I mean to hire a Depot-boy*
> *To carry me away."*

"Stop that singing and get down here!" yelled a shrieky, high-pitched voice with a British accent from the ground floor. Because the windows were open, Kate heard everything perfectly. Could that be Widow Smith? The singing stopped and one of the girls upstairs started laughing defiantly.

A carriage went by and the driver, a man in a top hat and coat, looked at Kate with a harsh face. She felt awkward standing in the street just staring at a building, so she made herself step forward to knock on the door. Just then a clear soprano voice sang out alone:

"Come all ye weary factory girls,
I'll have you understand,
I'm going to leave the factory
And return to my native land."

"Maureen Galligan! I know that's you. Stop that racket and get down here! Who's that at the front door!"

The shrieky voice sounded even louder. The door opened and a short, square woman with dark eyes faced Kate. "What do you want?" she shouted.

"I, ah, um, the conductor on the train told me to come see you, ma'am," said Kate nervously. "I've need of work and a place to stay."

The short woman looked annoyed at first, but then she seemed to have a change of heart. "Come in," she said, opening the door wide. She stalked over to the stairway and yelled upstairs in her hideous voice, "Galligan! Bring down your trunk! I've had enough of your rebelliousness! You'll have to find another place!"

And so it was that only eight hours after she overheard Patrick tell Nora they would be married, Kate found herself with a bed and a job in Lowell, Massachusetts.

"Keep your room clean and don't get involved with radicals," said Widow Smith as she led her upstairs to a small room with two double beds and four girls who were just finishing getting dressed. "Galligan, get out. I'm sending this new girl to the mill in your place. Hah! Maybe we'll have a little peace and quiet around here now."

Kate averted her eyes so she wouldn't have to look at

the pretty, bright face of the redheaded girl whose bed and job she was taking. The three other girls in the room didn't say a word. Kate wondered how they felt. Scared of the housemistress, that much she could tell.

Miss Galligan left with Widow Smith screaming at her all the way down the stairs. Kate stood nervously in the corner of the small room. Finally one of the other girls spoke. "My name is Laura Martin." She had a Maine accent, saying "Mah-tin" instead of "Martin." "I reckon you'll be working with us in Spinning Mill Number Twenty-three."

"Hello, I'm Kate O'Hara. Sure, I'm sorry about that other girl."

"So you're Irish too, eh? You don't seem Irish." Laura sighed snobbishly. "Well," she said and then seemed to change her mind about going on. She smoothed the quilts on her bed and left the room.

Factory bells started ringing out all over the city.

" 'Tis time to be leaving, Kate," said one of the other girls. She was short, thin, and plain-looking. "Quick now, on with your apron."

Kate quickly undid her shawl and took out her apron. The short girl's accent was Irish, and Kate was relieved to hear it.

"That all y' brought with you?" she asked.

"Aye," said Kate.

"You're as bad off as I was when I first arrived," she said, smiling. "I had been working as a domestic for an old ship's captain with one eye. He got too familiar, if y' know what I mean. I had no choice but to run away."

Kate didn't know what to say. She followed the girl down the stairs in a daze. The others had gone on ahead.

"That was two years ago," said the girl. "And by the way, my name is Mary Flannigan."

The girls walked along the canal, joining hundreds of other girls and women coming out of other boarding-houses. All along the canal were small bridges. At each bridge some of the girls left the procession and crossed over.

"Which mill are we going to?" asked Kate.

"That far one, three bridges down," answered Mary.

"Will I really have a job?" asked Kate. "Will they like me?"

"For certain you'll have a job," said Mary. "Widow Smith is Overseer Smith's sister. And as for liking you, you better not want too much of that. Just work fast and mind your own business. Don't worry. The overseer will be glad to be rid of Maureen."

"What will happen to her?"

Mary shrugged her shoulders. "I don't know. She's always speaking up for workers' rights and getting herself into trouble. I liked her myself, but I tried to stay away from her. I suppose she'll find a mill someplace where they haven't heard of her."

Kate felt something rebellious stir within at Mary's words, but she didn't want to care about anybody so she dismissed the feeling. They had reached the third bridge and were crossing it. They entered the factory.

The overseer, a balding, thin man with spectacles, looked Kate up and down and grunted with satisfaction when he learned that she was to replace Maureen Galligan.

"I don't want any more of her type, you hear? It was bad enough when those Yankee ladies organized the Female Labor Reform Association five years ago. We got rid of most of those girls, but that Maureen Galligan, why you'd have thought she was a Yankee herself, the way she carried on."

Kate felt her temper start to rise. But she couldn't let it get the best of her. Not now. She needed this job.

"You understand? No singing, no grievance committees, no turnouts, you hear?"

"Aye, sir," said Kate, hating the meekness in her voice.

The machine she was given to work on was a different kind of spinning machine, but Kate caught on quickly. Basically the work was the same. She had to watch for breaks, repair them, and replace bobbins the minute they became full. She was glad for the monotony of the work and relieved after the tension of the trip to lose herself in the numbing roar of the machinery.

Patrick, Mommy, Daddy, Mother O'Hara. Patrick, Mommy, Daddy, Mother O'Hara. Patrick, Mommy, Daddy, Mother O'Hara. The names of the people she loved became a chant that blended in with the clacking and whirring of the spinning machines. She didn't know what she was invoking by saying them, but she said them over and over all day long until at last they began to mean nothing to her. The sounds of the machines and her words were one, and she was lost in a knot-tying trance.

Days passed. She kept herself carefully detached and separate. She just ate, slept, and worked. The other girls talked about workers they'd known who came to Lowell to work and hated it so much that they jumped into the canals and drowned. Kate listened to the stories, but no matter how depressed she was, she wouldn't consider taking her own life. No, the way out for her was to numb herself so much that she no longer cared about anything.

Mary was friendly, but Kate didn't want a friend. During meals at the boardinghouse she spoke only when spoken to. She didn't read newspapers. She worked and slept. She stopped having complete thoughts. Whenever she thought about Lancaster, she said the numbing chant. Patrick, Mommy, Daddy, Mother O'Hara. She was like a wooden spindle in the machine. A cog. A no one. A person without a self.

And that was how she wanted it.

Each night the other girls went to lectures offered for the improvement of the workers' minds. Mary especially was trying to educate herself. One night she tried persuading Kate to attend a talk about Pueblo Indians. Kate wasn't interested.

"Leave me be, please," she pleaded. "I'm too hot and tired. I must sleep."

"That's the trouble with you!" said Mary. "Y' don't want to hear about anything! All y' do is sleep, eat, and work. Sure, I know how you feel because I felt the same way when I first came here. But, lass, you have to get involved! There are opportunities for improvement here."

"I don't care," said Kate, and she didn't.

"Don't you even want to learn how to read?"

"I know how to read."

"Ah, then ye won't be needing me to read this letter."

"What letter?" Kate opened her eyes. Mary was smiling and holding a letter in her hand.

"Where did you get that?"

"Widow Smith. She told me to give it to you."

Kate sat up. "Give it to me!" She looked at the envelope. It was from Uncle Mick. She tore it open and read:

Dear Kate,

Surely, we were shaken to find you gone, and we still don't know what to make of it. Patrick guessed you might have gone to Lowell and asked the conductor on the Boston train if he had seen a girl like you. He was told you might be living now at a boardinghouse run by the conductor's cousin. I surely hope this letter finds you there.

Clare, Bridget, and Michael miss you sorely. Ever since Patrick found out where you went, he won't speak of your leaving. God bless you, Kate, did ye leave because of higher wages there? Did y' feel you didn't have a place anymore in the family what with Patrick and Nora going to be married? I understand, lass, and am sure they will take loving care of the children.

Ye may wonder about the round-trip train ticket in this letter. Despite plans for his wedding, Patrick seems more grievous than ever about the death of his mother. I know how pleased he will be if at least all his brothers

and sisters are here on the special day. You can return
the train fare when you're more settled there. The wed-
ding is next Sunday at 8:00 A.M. at your house.
    Take care, Kate, and God love you.

                                            Your affectionate,
                                            Uncle Mick

Kate threw the letter to the floor and sobbed. Mary
discreetly picked it up and put it in the new trunk Kate had
bought.

I could never go back there! It would kill Patrick to see
me and it would kill me to see him. It's impossible. Oh,
God, why did you ever let this happen to me?

Kate wept into her pillow and fell asleep before the
others came up to bed.

The next day and succeeding days Kate resolved to rip
up the ticket, but she never did. Time passed in a death-
like rhythm of sleep and work, sleep and work. Kate tried
not to think about the wedding, and most of the time she
was successful, but every day when the wake-up bell rang,
her first thought was to name the day and her second
thought was to count the number of days to the wedding.
She would then click her mind closed and proceed
through the day without a further thought about it. Gradually she convinced herself she no longer cared.

But when the morning came when she said, "Saturday.
One more day," she found to her dismay that she couldn't
turn off her feelings so neatly.

She was heartbroken, lonely, jealous, and furious.
There was no hope that she would ever feel any better.

She dressed quickly, nodding politely at Mary's chatter and ignoring the other girls, who never spoke to her anyway. When she reached into her trunk for her apron, she put her hand on the ticket.

If she was to use it, she would have to leave that night right after work. A train for Boston left then. She'd heard mill girls mention it. Kate grabbed the ticket and shoved it in her apron pocket.

I'll just take it to work with me so that in some small way I'll feel close to Patrick, she persuaded herself as she hurried downstairs after Mary. At breakfast she kept one hand over her pocket. But of course I won't use it. I'll just keep it with me today and tomorrow. It's the only link to him I have.

All day at work she repeated to herself, I won't use it. But the fact was, she *was* going to use it, and she must have known it on some level because she had worn the new dress she had bought with her first wages and she was feeling more alive than she'd felt since she'd arrived. Her mind was working again. It had to. It had to find a reason she could accept for going home.

All day long she worked and thought. She worked faster than she'd worked since she'd arrived, and the overseer stopped by to say so.

"Miss O'Hara, I've been noticing that you seem to be adjusting to Lowell. It always takes the girls a few weeks." It was the first time he had spoken to her since her first day.

"Thank ye, sir," she said, wondering why she continued

to keep her Irish accent. At least half the girls in Lowell were Yankees from the hills of Maine, Vermont, Massachusetts, and New Hampshire. Apparently the mills in Lowell had once been full of them. But now that there were so many potato famine immigrants from Ireland willing to work under any conditions, the Yankee girls were leaving the mills in disgust. They didn't like the Irish. The girls who stayed in the mills were the ones who had no homes to go home to. They formed cliques and acted superior.

Kate was put off by the snotty workers. Her heart went out to the Irish girls, who for the most part were ignorant and intimidated. Maureen Galligan had been an exception. Perhaps Kate could be another. Even if she was withdrawn in Lowell, she could still give the impression she was both Irish and intelligent.

Patrick would have understood. He would have sympathized with the Irish girls and tried to help them. For a moment Kate stopped working and looked around the room. That was it! That was the bargain she'd been subconsciously searching for all day. If she could see Patrick one more time, then she would return to Lowell and do something worthwhile with herself. She would do what Patrick would do, help these girls organize a union.

In the midst of the huge, noisy machines Kate suddenly felt important. Maybe that's why she'd been sent back in history. To help these girls get used to the United States. She was part of a plan. Whose plan? Who was she striking a bargain with?

Maybe it was her heart. Maybe it was God.

Mother O'Hara's words came back to her. "For sure, it's a queer world, Kate."

It didn't matter how queer it was or who the other bargainer was. Now that the deal was set, she wasn't interested in details. She was going to see Patrick again. That's all she cared about.

18

Kate was suddenly giddy. Her fingers flew about, doing their job nimbly on their own, while she thought of the work she might do and, most of all, of Patrick. Her heart pounded and time passed quickly. Before she knew it she was at the train station and on the train to Boston.

There she had to wait several hours for the local Hartford train that would stop in Lancaster, but she didn't care. She found a day-old newspaper and sat on a bench and read every word with renewed interest. She felt a part of the world again. She read about a convention the southern states had just held in Nashville during which they decided not to leave the union. Not yet, she thought, feeling once again the power of knowledge she had not yet begun to use. She read the help wanted columns, fuming whenever she saw an ad that described a job and then said, "No Irish need apply." She thought again of John Fitzgerald Kennedy, who would someday be born in Massachusetts.

When her train departed, she was on it. She was so excited about the thought of seeing Patrick again that she sat straight up all the way to Lancaster. Sometimes she caught herself smiling as if she were actually sitting across from him. She had to put her hand up to her lips so other passengers wouldn't think she was odd.

When the train pulled into Lancaster at seven A.M., Kate stepped down trembling. She looked around expectantly, half-hoping Uncle Mick would be waiting for her. But the station was empty.

Kate watched the train depart in a cloud of steam, staring at the smoke until the last of it disappeared into the blue sky.

She took a deep breath and was surprised to hear herself sob. She realized she must look awful. Her hands were dirty. Her dress was wrinkled and messy. The wedding didn't start for an hour. She had no money.

This was stupid. She should never have come. It was an utterly foolish thing to do.

She went over her plans, trying to find reassurance in them. She had an hour to wait. Only an hour. Then she would walk home and peek in the side window to see the wedding. She would take just one look. That was all. She would bother no one. Then she would walk back to the train station and take the nine o'clock train back to Boston.

Kate sat on a bench and tried to still her heartbeat. The plan will work, she tried to convince herself. She took off her bonnet and redid her hair as best she could. She picked up a straw and cleaned her fingernails. She spit on a corner of her shawl and washed her face.

Time passed at an agonizingly slow pace. She redid her hair and cleaned her fingernails again. When she thought an hour had passed, she made herself wait even longer. Then she couldn't sit still any longer. Everyone will be inside now. It must be time to go. I'll walk down the street as though everything were perfectly normal. If I meet anyone, I'll say hello, I came back for my brother's wedding.

But I won't go in. No. I'll just look in the window quickly, then hurry back to the train station.

Trembling, she walked to their house. Halfway down she saw a red wagon with "Daguerreotype Saloon" written on it in fancy gold letters. Kate knew that was a kind of photographer because her mother was always talking about the "haunting beauty" of old daguerreotype pictures. What a lot of nerve Nora has, thought Kate, hiring a photographer when she *has* to get married.

She walked faster down the street, half hoping someone would see her and cry out, "Look who's here!" How she longed to hug Bridget, Michael, Clare, and . . . but no one came.

As Kate got nearer to the house she took a deep breath and crossed the yard around to the side window. She picked up her skirt and stepped behind a large bush. She was well hidden now. At first she couldn't bring herself to look in the window. Then she just had to.

Her heart stopped. Patrick and Nora were standing to one side of the parlor with Father Tully. Nora wore a beautiful new blue dress. Patrick had on his old suit, the same one he had worn the first day Kate had seen him. Kate wiped her tears away to get a better look at him. His hair was plastered down with water but chunks of it were starting to stick up. In spite of how awful she felt Kate had to smile. Poor Patrick. He was staring at the floor. Nora was smiling innocently and gazing up at him like a cow. Father Tully was looking at someone, and the room was quiet, as if everyone was waiting for something to happen.

"It's all right, Patrick. I'm here. I understand," whispered Kate. "Take good care of yourself and the children. Don't worry about me. I'm going to help the workers in Lowell, Patrick. That's what you would do, isn't it?"

"Patrick!" It was Clare's voice. Kate's heart leaped to hear it. "Look at the camera!"

Suddenly Patrick raised his head and looked straight out the window at her. It was as if he had sensed the whole time she was there because he knew right where to look. For a full moment they stared at each other, Kate willing her tears not to cloud her vision. She tried to smile, and then a blinding flash went off.

She felt herself fall. Down, down she went through space until she landed full force on her back. She lay still and gasped. She couldn't get her breath. Her chest ached. Her lungs wouldn't open. Once, when she was little, she had fallen off a swing and had not been able to breathe then either. Kate heaved her shoulders against the ground to make her lungs open up. She gasped, realizing she was going to fall again, and dug her fingers into the smooth percale sheet beneath her. She grabbed her pillow tightly and screamed.

"Patrick!"

"Kate! What's the matter?"

She heard someone run upstairs. Her real mother, the one with short brown curly hair, so young-looking—she had never realized how young-looking—this mother burst into her bedroom and looked around.

"Why did you scream?"

"Oh, God, Mother, it's you," Kate whispered.

"Kate, what's wrong with you? I swear, you've been acting so strange lately, I'm thinking of calling Dr. Rhodes."

Kate's mother came over and sat on the edge of Kate's bed. Kate threw her arms around her and felt her mother's body tense. Then, after a moment's hesitation, her mother relaxed and put her arms around Kate too.

Kate shut her eyes. Patrick! I still want to see you! she thought, but she loved the soft velour touch of her mother's bathrobe and the smell of shampoo in her mother's hair.

"Is there something you want to tell me, Kate?" asked her mother gently.

Kate opened her eyes and looked at the room around her. It was completely redecorated. The ceiling was white, the curtains were white, the floors had been sanded and polyurethaned, the walls were covered with beige wallpaper that had a tiny white floral print on it. On the walls were old photographs. Kate stared. One of them was a photo of Patrick and Nora in their wedding clothes.

"Where did you get that?"

"What, dear?"

"That picture!" Kate ran over and pointed to it.

"Why, Kate, you picked that one out yourself just yesterday. Don't you remember? What's the matter with you?"

Kate grabbed the photograph off the wall. Nora was still smiling at Patrick. Patrick's hair was still wet and sticking up. He was still looking right at her.

"Who are they?" Kate managed to ask, even though she knew.

"Oh, Kate, I told you yesterday!" Her mother sighed impatiently. "Oh, all right, for the last time, they are your great-great-grandparents, Nora and Patrick O'Hara. As I said, I don't know much about her, but Patrick was the first Irishman to buy land in the North End. He built a boardinghouse on Galway Street where your great-grandmother grew up. They had five children, one of whom was my grandmother. Then he left."

"Left?"

"They said he went to California to take a cure. Nora kept the boardinghouse going and raised the children all by herself. A tough, admirable old lady, she was."

"Cure for what?"

Kate's mother shrugged her shoulders and laughed. "Well, it's hard to tell. It could have been TB—or consumption, as it was called in those days—but I always thought by the way my grandmother spoke of him that it must have been alcoholism."

Kate held the picture close to her breast and lay back on the bed. *Mavourneen dheelish*, he had called her.

"I think I'll just sleep a little more," she whispered.

"Fine, dear, but don't forget, you're going to help me paint later."

"Okay."

"Maybe we'll go to Le Factory for lunch when we're finished."

Kate sighed. "I think I'd rather go to McDonald's today," she said.

"Well, all right," said her mother. "Shall I put the picture back?"

"No," said Kate.

Her mother crossed the room, stopped at the door, and looked back. "Are you sure you're all right?"

"Yeah, I just had a weird dream," said Kate in a purposely low-key voice. "I dreamed I went back in history and fell in love with the boy in this picture."

"I see, so that's it," said her mother with a chuckle.

"Well, go back to sleep for an hour and have some more fun. I'll call you when I'm finished spackling."

"He lived in this house," said Kate.

"Really? I don't think so, dear. That would be just too much of a coincidence, wouldn't it? Now you just rest and I'll wake you later."

"It was a factory house," whispered Kate. "Halfway down Paddy Lane."

But her mother was already downstairs.

About the Author

Jean Marzollo was raised in Manchester, Connecticut, a suburb that was originally a mill town. She remembers being taken by her mother to the Irish section and hearing tales about her great-grandfather, who had worked at the mill when it was thriving and who was the first Irishman in the town to buy his own land.

When Ms. Marzollo became interested in using Manchester's past as the background for her novel, she began to research the cloth mills that dotted New England during the nineteenth century. The material she uncovered was rich and fascinating. As she says, it convinced her even more strongly that "history, after all, is the best story we have."

Ms. Marzollo has written several books of nonfiction for adults. Her picture books include *Uproar on Hollercat Hill* and *Amy Goes Fishing*. This is her first novel for young adults. She lives with her husband and two sons in Cold Spring, New York.